FISH

You could say that Floss was the first real pos-
session Jimmy Barnes—nicknamed 'Fish'—had
ever had. The leggy, mongrelly animal seemed as
out of place in the Welsh village as the bony,
awkward boy, so it was not surprising that the
two should want to stick together from the start.
Fish's birthday, his desk at school, and even his
first name all belonged to someone else, which is
how he came to be called Fish in the first place,
and why he wanted Floss so badly that he was
driven to seek refuge with the dog in the hills in
winter-time, when Floss's life looked like being
in danger.

FISH

BY ALISON MORGAN
Illustrated by John Sergeant

CHATTO and WINDUS

Published by
Chatto and Windus Ltd.
42 William IV Street
London W.C.2.

*

Clarke, Irwin and Co Ltd
Toronto

First Impression 1971
Second Impression 1973

ISBN 0 7011 0467 8

Printed in Great Britain by
Redwood Press Limited
Trowbridge, Wiltshire

To Richard

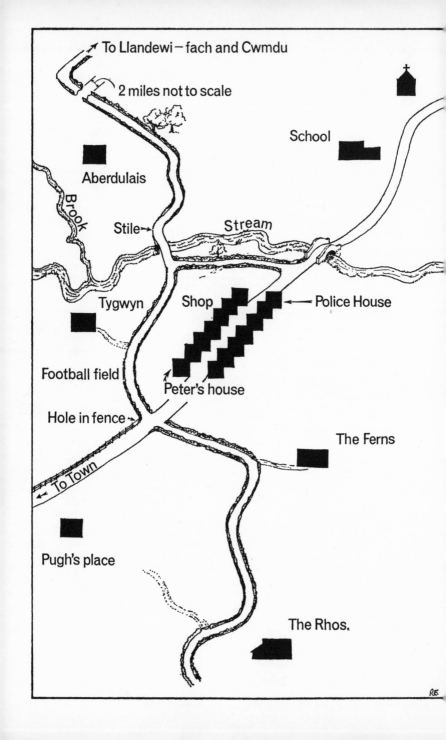

Chapter 1

'GOAL!' shouted Pete.

It was, too. I tried to stop the ball, but tripped over a mole-hill, and fell flat on my face in the mud.

'Trust Jimmy,' said Tom, but he did not really sound cross. Tom's good in that sort of way. It was just Tom and I playing against Pete and Tom's younger brother Gary, and we badly needed that goal, because it had been two all, and the light was fading. Very soon Tom's mum would shout to the boys to go in for tea and Pete and I would have to go home, too. It was all right for Pete because he had his bike, and it would only take him three minutes to coast down the hill into the village, and his mother never seemed to mind what time he got in. It took me nearly twenty minutes to get back up to our farm, and Mum would grumble at me for being out on my own in the dark. Still, that could not be helped; if I was the one who had let that goal through I couldn't break off the game first.

'Come on!' I said. 'Our kick-off. Give us that ball, Fish.'

Fish was mooching about on the touch-line. There was no touch-line, really, but we reckoned the pitch ended somewhere along the edge of the smoother bit of the field, just before it got boggy and clumpy with rushes. Even the smooth bit wasn't very smooth, and Gary must have been thinking the same thing.

'There's too many flippin' mole-hills,' he said, jumping on one and trampling it into a flat circle of red earth, while we waited for Fish to throw us the ball. He hopped along with that funny uneven way of running that he has, and picked it up.

'Oh, it's dirty!' he exclaimed, and dropped it again. We couldn't help laughing, but I was impatient, too.

'Oh, come *on*, Fish,' I said, running towards him. He gave it a feeble sort of kick that only moved it about four yards, and I ran to pick it up.

'Heck, and you are!' cried Fish. 'Can you see yourself?' I looked down at my jeans. Well, of course they were muddy. You can't play football in a wet field without getting muddy.

'And your face!' Fish went on. 'I'd like to see your mum when she catches sight of you. She won't know who you are. I bet she'll be mad.'

Nobody took much notice. We wanted to get on with the game before it got too dark. Tom took the kick-off, and I tried to find space, but Pete was too quick for me. Away down the field he went, with Gary sprinting along as fast as his little legs would carry him, so as to be there when Tom tackled, to take the ball from Pete and score a final decisive goal. But it did not happen, because Tom tackled too well and too soon. I was ready for the pass from Tom. Somewhere in the background I could hear Fish's voice, shrill with excitement, asking if I didn't think my dad would leather me. Silly fool. Why did he come and watch us playing football if he wasn't interested in the game?

Here comes the ball. It will be slippery, and heavy with mud. I've got it though, nicely between my toes, and away as fast as I dare over the rough ground. Pete is bearing down on me, and he's so much bigger than me, and faster. Gary's fast, too, although he's so little for his age, but luckily he puffed himself out before when he ran down hoping to score. Now there's Tom, striding across through the gloom. I'd rather try and get the goal myself, but better not risk it. Pete's almost on me, so—away to Tom, and with one good hefty kick, the ball sails between the goal-posts—my anorak, that is, and Pete's blazer.

'That was a good pass, Jimmy,' said Tom. I'd like to have said it was a good kick, but I thought it would sound silly, because Tom is twelve, two years older than me.

'Jolly good goal,' shouted Fish, and clapped. It did sound silly, so I was glad I hadn't said anything.

Just then, Tom's mother came out and called them in for tea. I think if it had just been Pete and me she would have asked us to come in for tea too, but with Fish hanging about it was a bit awkward, so she did not say anything. Perhaps it was just as well, because then I really would have been late home.

Tom and Gary went into the farmhouse, and Pete went round by the yard to get his bike. My quickest way was not to go through the farmyard and round by the lane, but straight across the field to the corner, which was actually just by the cross-roads. Pete would come up the lane to the cross-roads and then turn left and down the main road into the village, but my way home took me across the main road and up the lane on the other side. At first, although narrow and winding, it was not too steep and had a smooth surface like any other road, but after passing the Fern Cottages it became just a rough farm track, clambering up steeply for three-quarters of a mile until it reached our little farm right away up at the top of the dingle.

Everybody who comes to see us for the first time says, 'But don't you get terribly snowed up in the winter?' and of course we do, but I don't mind that. It's silent and exciting when it's full up with snow.

When Pete and I leave Tygwyn—that's Tom's farm—at the same time, I always run across the field to try and beat him to the cross-roads.

'Come on!' I said to Fish. 'If we run, we'll see Pete at the corner.' Fish started to run, but soon stumbled to a walk, picking his way clumsily through the clumps of rushes that grow thick at that end of the field.

'Wait for me!' he called. I jogged on, because I could hear Pete ringing his bell as he swung out of the yard on to the lane and I knew if I went all out I could do it. But then I stopped and waited. After all, there wasn't much point in busting myself just to get a glimpse of Pete when I'd been playing football with him all afternoon. It was just a habit I had got into—something to break the alone-ness of the long trail home. This time there was Fish to keep me company, for what that was worth. As soon as he caught me up, I jogged on to the corner, and slipped between the pig-netting and the strand of barbed wire that ran along the top. I'd been doing that for years, and I suppose getting bigger all the time, because there was a well-worn sagging gap that just seemed to fit me. It came as natural, slipping through that gap, as pulling on an old pair of gumboots at the back door. But Fish went and caught his anorak, and ripped it—how, I don't know, because he's much thinner than me—only a little tear, not more than an inch each way from the corner, but he was in a real fuss about it.

'I knew it was silly to come this way,' he said. 'We should have gone round. It's all your fault.'

I told him not to be daft, and I hadn't asked him to come with me. Anyway, he'd think twice about going the long way round if he lived right up at the Rhos, like I did, instead of only at the Ferns.

'You pulled the wire as I was going through,' he said.

'I did *not*.' I wasn't even near him. What would I want to do a silly thing like that for? But it was the kind of thing Fish would do, so maybe he thought everyone else acted that way. I was just about to say that when I saw he was crying. That shook me a bit. Maybe I'd cry if I'd torn my finger on some barbed wire, but not my clothes.

'What's the matter, Fish?' I said. 'Will your mother be very cross?'

'I don't know. I'm scared she'll tell my dad.'

My dad wouldn't think the state of my clothes any business of his, except just to tell me to go and get changed if I'd come in wearing my school trousers and he wanted me out on the farm. Anyway, his own working clothes were always in tatters. 'Only held together by dirt,' Mum would say.

'If she does tell him, what would he do?' I asked. 'Give you a hiding?'

'Oh, I don't know,' said Fish. 'Maybe. Maybe nothing. Maybe go on about it.'

That did not sound worth crying about. Mum often goes on at me, but she does not really mind. When she gets into her stride about me getting so filthy, and so untidy, and so late, and all that, Dad just sits quiet in a corner, and after a while he winks at me. If Mum catches him at it, she turns round and starts on him, and then I wink at him, and then we all start laughing, and Mum says, 'You men! You're all as bad as each other.'

We crossed the main road and were just starting up our lane when something caught Fish's eye.

'Look,' he said, 'a dog.' I stepped back and glanced up the

main road. A leggy mongrelly sort of animal was bounding down the road towards us, but when it got about six feet away it stopped and cringed, wagging its tail and looking guilty all at the same time, like sheepdogs often do when they can't be sure whether you are going to hit them or pat them. Only this wasn't a sheepdog, or at least most of it wasn't. It was some kind of hairy long-legged terrier, very dirty and very thin.

'I've never seen that dog before,' I said. 'It doesn't live around here.'

Fish held out his fingers. 'Here, boy,' he said. 'Come on then.' The animal edged itself forward on its tummy, its tongue going in and out, and its tail sweeping across the tarmac, but cautious. Its ears kept flickering up and down—up for anxiety, down flat for love and affection. I went to stroke it, and it flew off up the road.

'You've frightened it,' said Fish.

'Not for long,' I answered, and the dog soon came back, squirming round us in a circle, keeping just out of reach. Fish stayed crouched down, and after a while the dog came close enough to sniff at his elbow. Fish slowly put out his other hand and after letting the dog sniff his fingers he ran them gently up the side of its nose. Suddenly the dog went wild with excitement. It threw itself all over Fish, licking his face, scratching his precious anorak with its dirty paws, pressing its muddy body against him.

Fish, surprisingly, didn't seem to mind. He made a few feeble efforts to keep the dog down, but he loved it really.

'Down, dog,' he said, and it rolled over on its back, then up again. I noticed it was a bitch, and said so.

'Is he?' said Fish.

'She,' I said.

'Is she?' he asked. 'How do you know?'

It's funny the things Fish doesn't know. I suppose it comes of spending most of his life in a town. At least, I wasn't sure where he had lived, because according to Fish he had lived in a lot of places, but his family had only been at the Ferns for three months, and they weren't ordinary country people like the rest of us, and yet they weren't exactly towny either. They were the kind of people who did not seem to belong anywhere.

I told Fish how I knew she was a bitch, and he seemed quite interested, but then his mind went on to the next thing.

'Do you think she belongs to anyone?' he said.

'She must belong to *somebody*,' I said.

13

'Perhaps she's just a stray,' said Fish. He hugged her tight. I went to stroke her, but she still seemed a bit nervous of me, and backed away.

'She likes me best,' said Fish.

'She's made you very dirty,' I retorted. 'What will your dad say now?'

'Oh, I'll say one of the boys rolled me in the ditch,' said Fish. 'That will explain how it got tore, too.'

I thought that was a bit mean, but Fish was like that. You could never trust him. He'd think up any kind of story rather than take the blame for something himself.

Fish had been sitting quiet, hugging the dog. 'I'm going to keep her,' he said. He sounded frightened, yet defiant.

'You can't,' I said. 'Somebody will claim her.'

'Who?' said Fish.

'Whoever she belongs to.'

'I don't think her owner wants her any more. I think she's just been abandoned.'

'How do you mean, abandoned?' Of course you have to drown puppies just like kittens if nobody wants them, but I didn't see how you could just turn out a half-grown dog like this one. It would come back again, anyway. All the same, if ever I saw an unwanted-looking dog, this was it. Except that Fish wanted it, wanted it very badly.

'She's getting big enough to need a licence,' said Fish. I did not know much about that, because none of our dogs need licences, being working sheepdogs, but this one looked kind of half-dog, half-puppy age, daft and fun like a puppy, but almost as big as a full-grown dog.

'There's lots of dogs abandoned when they get old enough to need a licence,' Fish went on. 'It's easy, say, if you're moving house. You just leave the dog behind.'

'How do you know?' I asked. 'I bet you're just making it up because you want to keep her.'

'It's true, anyway,' said Fish. 'I know because—I just know.'

I stared at the dog, trying to think of somebody she might belong to, but I could not think of anyone. I knew just about every household for two or three miles around, and pretty well all the dogs, too. They were mostly sheepdogs, of course, at all the farms, and one or two corgis. Some of the small houses in the village itself had a dog kept as a pet, but they were all small terriers or things like that; nobody had a dog as big as this one, or one that looked as forlorn.

'Would they let you keep it at home?' I asked. The more I learnt about Fish's parents, the less they seemed the sort of people who would let Fish have a dirty stray mongrel to look after; and what about the licence?

Fish did not answer that. 'I'm going to keep her anyway,' was all he said.

'How?' I asked. It really was getting dark now, and I wanted to get back home. 'If you're sure it will be all right, we can start up, but if not we'd better take her to Tygwyn and they can ring up the police station.'

'I'll *make* them let me keep her,' said Fish, and he sounded quite bold and fierce. I couldn't see how he was going to do that, but at least it meant we could get moving.

'Come on then,' I said. 'Hey, you dog, you come with us.'

Fish tried to whistle to her, to show she was his dog, not mine; he wasn't very good at whistling, but she followed us all the same.

'We must give her a name,' he said.

'She has probably got one,' I said. 'Anyway, I'm sure you will find someone claims her.'

'They won't know I've got her,' said Fish quickly. I stopped and looked at him.

'Oh yes, they will,' I said. 'We'll call in at Tygwyn tomorrow and ask them to ring the police station. It would be stealing otherwise.'

Fish was about to argue, but then he stopped and thought for a bit.

'Tell you what,' he said. 'I'll let you ring the police to-morrow if you'll do something for me now.'

'What's that?' I asked.

'I'm going to tell my dad that she was found straying at Tygwyn and Mr Thomas' (that's Tom's father), 'asked me to look after her till they found the proper owner.'

'What's the point of that?' I asked.

'Mr Thomas is our landlord. If Dad thinks Mr Thomas wants me to have her, he won't try to stop me.' It struck me that Fish's father must have a mind like Fish's if they both think in that funny round-about sort of way.

'It sounds a bit daft to me,' I said. 'Mr Thomas is bound to find out, and then what?'

'Perhaps he won't. But we needn't worry about that now.'

'Look,' I said. 'Why don't I take the dog on up with me to the Rhos? It won't make much difference having one extra dog up there and . . .'

'She's mine!' Fish interrupted fiercely. 'I saw her first. It's me she likes, not you. You shan't have her!'

I laughed, he flies up into such a silly rage about things. 'I'm only trying to be helpful,' I said. 'She can be yours, only we keep her at our place because it's easier. You can come and see her and play with her and that.'

'No!' he shouted. 'No, no, no!' There were tears in his voice, and he seized me round the wrists, clutching with bony fingers. 'You've got plenty of dogs of your own. This one's mine, mine, and you're not going to take her away from me. You take everything from me, and you're not going to take my dog.'

'Get off!' I said, shaking myself free. I was surprised at the strength of his grip, because he was pretty feeble in a mock-fight. 'What have I ever taken from you?' Gary and I have wrestling matches sometimes for something we both want, like the last toffee or the best conker, but that's always good fun. I've never fought Fish for anything; it would be like bullying. Anyway, he's never had anything I want.

16

Fish started walking very fast uphill. 'You've always taken everything that's mine,' he said.

'Such as what?'

'Such as my name, and my place in class, and . . . and my birthday.'

Well, that was daft. I thought he would have liked having the same birthday as me. It was only when the teacher asked, 'Who has a birthday this week?' and we both put our hands up that we discovered we were twins. The other boys were pretty surprised to discover Fish was going to be ten, because, as I say, you would never have thought it.

The fuss about his place in class was silly, too. Gary and I had always sat together ever since we first went to school, and then when Fish arrived, late in the summer term, the teacher put him to sit with Gary, because she said he was new and we should make him feel at home. I was a bit annoyed, and so was Gary, but it didn't matter much because I was only just across the way and Gary and I still managed to have a good bit of fun together. Anyhow, when the autumn term came round, I think Miss Davies must have felt it was a waste of time, and Fish was miles behind Gary in his work, so Gary and I were back together again and Fish was on his own.

'Don't be silly, Fish,' I said. 'I didn't take your birthday any more than you took mine, and I can't help it if we are both called Jimmy.'

'Wherever I've been, whatever school I've been to, there's always been another Jimmy who was there first. I've never been called by my own name—always some stupid nickname,' Fish muttered. He was getting puffed, trying to walk ahead of me and trying not to cry and he kept having to swallow to let the words get out.

When Fish had first turned up at school and said his name was Jimmy, everybody had tried to call him Jimmy for a time, but it was confusing. They called him Jimmy the Ferns, because he lived there, and that led to me being called Jimmy the Rhos. That was a bit aggravating for me; after all, every-

17

body had always known me just as Jimmy. However, it didn't last long. Fish was always boasting about what a good swimmer he was and how many medals he had gained in some swimming baths or other. Then a really hot spell came along, and all we boys spent the summer evenings in the stream. There's quite a good pool in one place, deep enough to swim in. Fish often used to mooch about on the bank, just like he does on the touch-line, but he always had some excuse or other for not going in the water. One day, when he was hanging about, Gary, who has a comical way of talking, suddenly shouted up at him, 'Come on, fish! Swim!' After that, he was always called Fish. The name suited him. He was an odd fish anyway.

'Fish,' I said, 'shall I try and call you Jimmy?' I knew I'd never be able to, but I could try.

'It wouldn't work,' he said. Some things Fish understood very well. We were almost at the Ferns now, and instead of struggling on with his back to me he turned and faced me. 'Stop a minute,' he said. All the way up, although he would not look right round at me, he had been glancing down sideways to make sure the dog was following, and now he put his hand on her neck. 'You've got to help me. You will help me, won't you?'

'Do what?' I said.

'Back me up when I tell Dad that Mr Thomas gave me the dog.'

'I don't see what it's got to do with me,' I said. 'I can't come in now anyway. It's awfully late and I shall be in trouble as it is.'

'*Please.* Dad'll believe you. He won't believe me.'

I felt very uncomfortable. I was being asked to tell a downright lie that wasn't going to do me any good, and was almost certain to be found out.

'You *promised*,' said Fish. 'When I agreed to let you ring the police tomorrow.'

I did not think that I had, but Fish had got me in such

a state of feeling that I owed him something, that I agreed.

'All right,' I muttered. I told myself that I need only stand beside Fish while he told his tale, and just sort of nod, or grunt, and I could pretend afterwards I had not really said anything definite.

At that moment the front door of the Ferns opened and we could see Mr Barnes outlined against the oblong of light. A child was wailing inside, and in the still damp air I could already catch that sour dank smell that always seemed to come from the Ferns. It was a shabby place at all times. There had originally been two cottages, but one had begun to fall down. The last tenant in the other one had patched up the fallen roof and kept chickens in it. After he had gone both cottages stood empty for a time before the Barneses moved in. They never seemed able to get rid of the smell of mouldiness and stale chicken manure. There were no chickens now, but on wet days Mrs Barnes used to hang up the nappies across the empty rooms where the chickens used to live, and what with the nappies, and the dirt, and the damp and the scrambling babies—two of them—and Mrs Barnes's cooking and Mr Barnes's Woodbines, and scraggly garden with the kitchen scraps at one end and the toilet at the other, everything and everyone that came out of the Ferns had the same kind of faint mixed-up smell clinging to them. You could smell it on Fish if you sat close to him in school although he never actually looked dirty, and indeed took much more trouble to keep clean than any of us.

'Is that you, James?' called Mr Barnes, harshly. Then he saw I was there, too. 'Why, it's Jimmy Price, isn't it?' he went on, in quite a different tone of voice. 'My word, you're growing into a fine boy. Seeing you in the dark there I thought you were your father. Hey James, when are we going to see you grow into a fine boy like Jimmy?' He made it sound as though it were all Fish's fault that he was not as tall as me.

I don't know any grown-up that I disliked talking to as much as Mr Barnes. He always spoke to me as though I were

20

an important grown-up whom he particularly wanted to impress, like Mr Thomas. I was sure he couldn't really be thinking of me in that way, so I knew it was just a sham, but what I could not understand was what he was getting at. I think really he was getting at Fish.

'Please, Dad,' said Fish.

'Well, what is it *now*?' said Mr Barnes, as though it were the sixtieth time Fish had asked him for something, when in fact it was the only thing he had said. 'Always whining for something, this boy is. You won't catch Jimmy Price whining for things, you may be sure of that.'

'Please Dad, I've got this dog.'

'*You've* got a dog? Don't be ridiculous.'

'It *is* mine. It's a stray, and . . .'

'You brought it here.'

'Yes. Because . . .'

'You found a dirty, filthy, stray dog from goodness knows where, and you brought it here. Why, may I ask?' It wasn't the kind of question Fish was meant to answer. 'Why you, and not Jimmy? I'll tell you. Jimmy has more sense than to pick up every disease-ridden thieving stray animal that he finds and take it into his nice clean house.'

'Mr Thomas Tygwyn gave it me.' Give Fish credit, he could tell a lie as though it were the truest, most matter-of-fact thing in the world. 'He found it hanging around the yard, and he's ringing the police to ask them if they can find the owner. He asked me if I'd look after it for him, seeing as we haven't got a dog. He was afraid it would fight with his dogs if he put it in the shed with them.'

It came over ever so natural. Fish sounded whining, but then he always sounded like that when he was talking to his father.

I began to move on up the hill. I hadn't actually said anything about the dog, but I had listened to Fish's tale without ever openly contradicting him, so I thought I'd done my share.

21

'You off home, Jimmy Price?' said Mr Barnes. 'I wish you could spare the time some day to teach my son to speak the truth. You just can't believe a word he says.' He turned to Fish. 'Be off indoors, you,' he said. 'I'll soon see this creature is sent about his business.'

I heard Fish give a little gasp and I knew that he was panicking. I was suddenly very angry, with a cold, grown-up sort of anger.

'Oh, dear,' I said. 'Perhaps I'd better take the dog home. Mr Thomas might be cross if he discovers Fish had turned it out after he had given it to him.'

Mr Barnes was flummoxed.

'Are you sure,' he said cautiously, after a pause, 'that Mr Thomas really meant James to bring the dog here?'

'Oh, yes,' I said airily. 'I was there when it happened. But Fi . . . James, can tell you all about it.' Let him see that, if he treated me as grown-up and trustworthy, then I treated Fish as grown-up and trustworthy.

Mr Barnes gave a tight sort of smile. 'I'm afraid James isn't always as truthful as I am sure you are,' he said.

'If you want to know exactly what happened then,' I said, 'we were just finishing a game of football in the field behind Tygwyn, when this dog appeared. We went into the yard to tell Mr Thomas, and the dog followed us. He said he was sure it was a stray, and he would find out who it belonged to. Then he turned to Fish—James—and said, "I'm sure your father won't mind if you keep the dog at your home for a few days, just until the owner turns up." I think he asked James because he's so good with animals, and he thought that as you haven't got any other dogs here. . . . But if you'd rather not, I'm sure my father would be willing to keep it up at the Rhos. We could try and see Mr Thomas didn't find out.' I didn't dare look at Fish. So long as it was just between me and Mr Barnes, I could almost believe myself.

'And what,' said Mr Barnes, 'if the owner doesn't turn up?'

He'd got a point there. 'Oh, I am sure Mr Thomas will deal with it,' I said.

Not, as Mr Barnes hastily explained, that he had anything against the dog, and it was most kind of Mr Thomas to have allowed James to have a pet for a few days, and he only wished they could keep it altogether, but of course the size of the house, and the small children, and his wife, and there being nowhere outside to keep the dog and . . .

For the time being, we had won. I said goodnight and went home, still without looking at Fish.

Chapter 2

I WENT very fast up the steep farm track, stumbling over the ruts in the darkness until I had no breath left. I stopped a moment, to ease the stitch in my side, and listened to the blood pumping in my ears, and then scrambled on again as quickly as I could. I really was going to be late home, but it wasn't that which worried me most. I wanted to get right away from the Ferns, to leave the nasty taste of the place behind, to get back into the embrace of the comfortable familiar smells of my own home—damp turf and the gurgling brook, cows and straw and diesel to greet me as I turned in at the yard, and inside the house the white smells of new milk and home-made lard and baking, and the richer brown smells of floor polish and frying sausages.

I wanted to forget the whole affair at the Ferns. I was angry with Fish, who had tricked me into doing something that seemed quite all right—even clever—at the Ferns, but made me go hot and cold with embarrassment when I realized that it was the same me who had told all those lies who would be walking into Tygywn tomorrow as an old friend of the family and saying . . . saying what? It was as though Fish had sucked me into his own dreary little world of sly make-believe and, like the smell of the Ferns, the memory of it would cling to me wherever I went. Before, Fish had been a bit of a nuisance, just because he did not belong to our world, the world of boys who had grown up together and were always free and welcome in each other's houses, and whose parents went to the same village parties, sang at the same concerts, enjoyed the same jokes; he was a nuisance because he was an outsider, but he hadn't really *mattered*. I did not want him to matter. Gary and Tom and Pete were my friends, and I certainly did not want to become an outsider like Fish.

I was home at last. I crossed the little yard of bare rock and kicked off my boots quietly in the porch. Then I carefully lifted the latch and slid into the kitchen.

Mum was at the sink, swilling out the milking things. My sister Jean was reading a comic, standing on one leg, like she does when Mum has just told her to put it away and be doing something else. Dan was sitting at the kitchen table dressed in his striped pyjamas and police hat—he always wears his police hat except when he's at school or chapel—eating porridge and looking all clean and pink from his bath.

'Sorry I'm late, Mum,' I said.

'I expect you're dirty as well as late, coming in so quiet and polite,' said Mum, before turning round. She finished wiping out a churn and then took a look at me. 'Yes,' she said, 'I was quite right.' I expect she would have wound herself up to say some more, but just then Dad came in behind me, and we did our winking act.

'Oh, well, now you're so late you might as well get into your pyjamas before supper,' she said.

'He can come up with me to the top field while he's like he is,' said Dad. 'I've been hedging down by the road all day, and I've not been round the ewes.'

'D'you want to go right up there with Dad, Jimmy?' She meant, wasn't I too tired, and I really was tired. We had been playing football all afternoon, and in the morning I had walked down to the village with Jean to get some groceries, and back up with the heavy basket. That was four times I had been up and down that steep mile to the main road, and a heap of running about as well. It would have been lovely just to be sitting down all clean and eating something hot, like Dan was doing.

'No, I'm not tired,' I said. 'I'll come with you.' You see, I'm the eldest, so it's our farm, really, Dad's and mine. At present, Dad does most of the work, and I just help a bit; one

25

day I'll do most of the work, and Dad will just help a bit, and the rest of the time he'll doze by the Rayburn like I remember Grandad doing before he died. Dad never says to me, you can't go and play football, you've got to come and help me, except of course at special times like harvest, and he doesn't have to say it then because all the boys help on all the farms in turn, anyway. But he wouldn't expect me to sit around at home doing nothing when there's work to be done.

We walked out across the yard and through the gate at the back on to the hillside. It was still and damp, and pitch dark by now, but though Dad had the big flash-lamp with him, he did not bother to switch it on yet. We knew our way around too well for that. At first the only sound was the spattering of the brook and the squelch of our boots in the strip of marsh you have to cross just there, but as we got up on to higher, dry ground and away from the stream we became aware of another sound.

'The sheep are making a lot of noise,' remarked Dad. The air was full of a blended humming sound which I knew as we got nearer would separate out into a chorus of bleats, some high, some low, some in the middle, like the sheep make at shearing-time when they are all huddled together in the yard.

'Do you think there's been a fox through the field?' I asked.

'Could be,' said Dad. 'But I don't think they'd make such a fuss about a fox. It's not as if it were lambing season.'

That was true. Except when the new-born lambs lay helpless in the fields the foxes and sheep did not bother much about each other.

'It's more like as if a dog's been among them,' said Dad uneasily, and he quickened his pace.

A dog that takes to worrying sheep has committed the unforgivable sin in the farming world. It's mostly sheepdogs that do it, of course, because it's mostly sheepdogs that live around the farms. People who keep dogs just as pets will say

26

they know their dog isn't the kind that would chase sheep, but farmers don't pay much heed to that sort of talk. It may be a long time before they get caught doing it, because dogs are canny, and they don't kill sheep on their own land, or next door, but maybe a mile away or more, and they don't do it all the time, but suddenly, when the mood takes them and the coast is clear, they'll slip off. If one or two farmers in a district find their sheep have been worried, or killed, then they know there's a sheep-killer around and that sheep-killing will go right on until the dogs responsible are discovered and shot.

The top field was hedged in, after a fashion, but that was all to distinguish it from the open mountain-side above. It was rocky and steep, and full of little springs, and had never felt the plough. As we pushed open the gate at the bottom, Dad swung the beam of light around from the flash-lamp. The sheep had quietened down, but when they saw the light they started up again, away off in the far corner. It was as we walked across the field towards them that the torchlight fell upon the dead sheep.

It was lying in a patch of bog below a spring, legs in the air, all torn and mangled. The wet moss and turf was churned up and muddy, as though there had been a tussle.

Dad bent down and felt her and lifted the lid over the staring eye. 'She's quite dead,' he said.

'Was it a dog?' I asked. I've seen dead sheep before, of course, but only ones that had been sick already. This seemed so brutal, and unnecessary. The sheep was still warm.

'I reckon so,' said Dad, grimly. 'Come on; we'd best go and look at the others.'

We walked on up to where the rest of the flock were huddled. They had gone quiet again when they heard our voices, and stood their ground, but uneasily. It would only have needed one to panic and the whole lot would have gone stampeding across to the other side of the field.

Dad stood still a little way off and ran his torch over them.

Their eyes gleamed green and alarmed in the light, and you could see their wet flanks steaming and heaving.

'I can't see any that are down,' Dad said. 'Can you, Jim?' I looked, but I couldn't see any.

'We'd better take a closer look at them, and count them if we can,' said Dad. 'If you'll try and shift them gently, I'll stand by here and check them as they go past.'

I did not think it was going to be very easy to get them to move gradually and not all in a rush, but sheep don't race about wildly in the dark like they do in the day-time. I walked along slowly, making soothing noises, while Dad stayed quietly where he was. I wanted to get them moving between him and the hedge, because that would stop too many of them going by in a lump. I knew if the first one or two went that way, then the rest would almost certainly follow. Sheep are like that.

It worked out all right. First the leader went along, stopping now and again to stamp, and I thought that the two that followed were going to plunge back when they caught sight of Dad standing there, but I waved my arms about and they thought better of it. I didn't dare shout in case it set the whole lot off again. After that, the others went by pretty smoothly. One, I thought, was limping.

'I think they're all there,' said Dad. 'I only made one short, and that will be the dead one. Still, we'd better walk round the hedges, because I could have easy made a mistake.'

We walked right round the field, and Dad said he had noticed one of the sheep had a bit of a gash on the shoulder. That must have been the one I saw limping. He said he thought that we had better try and get her down to the farm to have a proper look at it, afterwards.

We did not find any more sheep, though there were plenty of places in the corners where the ground was all trampled and churned up, as though the sheep had been rushing helter-skelter from one end of the field to the other and huddling together in the corners for protection.

Then we had to find the lame ewe and single her out from the others and catch her. That took some time, because she was not very lame, and by this time they were all thoroughly jumpy, and the longer we took to catch her the jumpier they became. Eventually we got her cornered, and I started driving her towards Dad who was waiting to nab her with his crook. But she suddenly took fright and bolted back straight at me. I clutched her by the wool and she started charging up the hill with me hanging on for dear life. If you've never held a sheep, you'll never believe how big and strong they are. Dad came running after, and between us we got control of her and half-carried, half-pushed her through the gate into the home field. After we got her away from the flock it was easy—she just let herself be driven gently down into the yard.

Dad told me to go on in and tell Mum he'd be in directly he had seen to the ewe. The gash was not too bad, but he thought it would be safer to put on some antiseptic and give her an injection. Bites can be nasty things.

I stood in front of the Rayburn peeling off my wet clothes while I told Mum what had happened. Then I left them in a heap on the floor and stumbled off to have a bath. 'And be quick,' Mum called. 'Supper's ready.'

I was quite quick because I was starving, and I knew if I lay still in the bath for two minutes I'd fall asleep. I was half-way through supper when Dad came in, and told much the same story as I had done. Jean and Dan were both in bed by this time.

'There's not been any sheep-killing round here for a long time,' he said, afterwards.

'You didn't see any dogs, of course?' asked Mum.

'No,' he said. 'And I haven't seen any strange dogs in these parts lately—have you, Jim?'

Then it clicked. Up to that moment, I honestly had not given another thought to Fish and his dog from the time I had walked in at the kitchen door earlier on. Even when we'd found the dead sheep, I hadn't thought anything. I was about to say why yes, of course, when I suddenly had a vision of Fish, clutching me with his bony fingers, and crying, 'She's mine! You take everything from me, and you're not going to take my dog!'

I knew if I told Mum and Dad about it, they'd be kind, and sorry for Fish, but firm. You can't save one dog at the cost of six or seven sheep, Dad would say, and it might be a great many more than that, once the dog got into the way of it. Of course, it wasn't for Dad to have the dog destroyed. That was a decision for Mr Barnes, but I knew Mr Barnes was unwilling enough to keep the dog in the first place. One breath that it might have been worrying sheep, and that would be the end of it.

'Have you, Jim?' repeated Dad. I must have been staring gormlessly into space while mechanically cleaning up the last of my baked beans.

'He's half asleep, bless him,' said Mum, as though she were talking about Dan. 'He'd tell you if he had, wouldn't you, Jimmy? You'd tell Dad if you'd seen any stray dogs.'

'Yes,' I muttered. That might mean anything.

'Off to bed, then,' said Mum. And I went, gladly.

Chapter 3

SOMETIMES something happens which seems so unimportant at the time that you don't pay any attention to it at all, but when the grown-ups get hold of it they make it grow and grow into a great affair and you think you'll never be able to live it down. Other times, you worry yourself sick over something you've done, thinking about the consequences, and nothing happens at all.

That was the way it was at the time of Fish and his dog. I got myself thoroughly bothered about my lies, and Mr Thomas, and the sheep-killing, and most of all about Fish and his dog, and I really did not know what I ought to do, or even what I wanted to do, but whatever I did I could see I was going to be in one heck of a mess. But in the event nothing happened at all—for the time being, that was. Later on, of course, it was a different story.

As a start, the next day was Sunday. That meant there was no particular need for me to see either Fish or any of the Thomases. The Thomases were church people, but we were chapel, so we went to different Sunday schools, at different times of day. Very often, as our Sunday school was in the afternoon, I would look in at Tygwyn on the way home, but they often went out visiting relations, so it wasn't a regular habit of mine. Fish scarcely ever came to Sunday school anyway. His father always blamed him, in front of me, for not going, but his mother said she had enough trouble getting him off in tidy clothes for school five days a week without having to do it again on Sunday. He must have been pretty bored, because he was always hanging about in the road as we came back, and would try to get us to stop and talk.

32

However, on this particular Sunday there was no sign of Fish or his dog either when we went down or when we came back. I knew I ought to go into Tygwyn to report the lost dog, but I told myself they were probably all out. I wanted to put it off as long as possible, but it was also awkward because I had Jean and Dan with me, and I had not mentioned anything about the dog to either of them.

On Monday, I really plucked up courage to go to Tygwyn. What made it easier was that Fish and I have to walk to school and back, but Jean and Dan go in the school car from the cross-roads, because they are younger. That meant I could call in with Fish on our way to school without them knowing. I was in a bit of a dither, but Fish seemed to have quite accepted his part of the bargain.

We met Mr Thomas in the yard. I explained about the stray dog—puppy, I called it—and he said he would certainly ring the police station for us.

'Where is it now?' he asked. 'Have you got it at your place, Jimmy?'

'Fish is looking after it,' I said, hastily.

'I've got it,' said Fish. 'Do you think it will be all right if I keep it until the police find the owner?' He was very cool.

'Finding's keepings,' said Mr Thomas. 'You keep it, that is if your father and mother don't object.'

How simple it was! Now, if Mr Barnes said anything to Tom's father about letting Fish have the puppy, it was all quite straightforward. Mr Thomas *had* said Fish could have it. They were unlikely to get to discussing times and dates. Mr Barnes rarely spoke to the other men in the neighbourhood. He always talked about Mr Thomas as though they were great friends, but you never saw him stopping by the roadside for an afternoon's chat, like the other men would.

The other, more serious matter of the sheep-killing, seemed to fizzle out, too. Normally, news gets around the village pretty quickly but sometimes an event falls through a gap in the network. That was what happened this time. I just said nothing about it at school and it so happened that neither Mum nor Dad had any reason to go down to the village or meet anyone, until they went to town on market day, which wasn't until the following Friday. So nobody knew we had had dogs after our sheep except us, and nobody at our place knew about Fish's dog, until at least a week had passed.

Of course Fish had been on at school about his wonderful dog, but nobody paid much attention to Fish's stories at any time, and we all had dogs at home anyway. Then, one day when we went out for morning break into the playground, there was Floss, swishing her tail back and forth across the asphalt, ears flat, pleading with Fish to be pleased to see her. I must say she looked a heap better than when I first saw her. I had been a bit afraid she might not get enough to eat, because though I knew almost nothing about Fish's mum, I couldn't see his father spending money on food for Fish's pet. But she looked lively, and clean, and well—not fat, because she was the skinny age anyway, all legs and bounce—but she had obviously been decently fed.

Fish made a great show of being surprised to see her. In fact, he sounded so surprised that I wondered whether he had left the door of the chicken house open on purpose, so that everyone would be able to see what a beautiful dog he had. If so, he must have been very sure she would follow him, and not stray off and get lost again.

He *was* very sure about his dog. I noticed especially, because the thing about Fish was that he never seemed to be sure about anything. But he seemed quite sure about Floss, and she was quite sure about him. He called her Floss—he had fixed on that without asking anybody, and she seemed to answer to it very well. All the children kept calling 'Floss! Floss! Come here, Floss! Good dog!' across the playground, and she would streak across from one to the other, once she had got over her shyness. But Fish only had to give his feeble little whistle and she would come to him, whoever else was calling.

She was a great success, and so, for the first time in his life, was Fish. Of course, as soon as our teacher saw her at the end of the morning break she said Fish must take her home, but she agreed he could leave her in the playground until the dinner-break, so as not to miss his lessons. But Floss just sat quietly in the porch all the time until the dinner-break, as good as gold, so then Miss Davies said that as she was no trouble, she could stay until the end of school.

That evening, Jean said at tea-time, 'We saw Fish's sweet little puppy today!'

Mum looked up. 'I didn't know Fish had a puppy,' she said.

'Oh, it's quite new,' said Jean. 'I think somebody gave it him, because he hasn't got any animals.' I don't know where Jean got her facts from—it wasn't from me. I was just about to put her right, which is something I am often having to do, because she's always talking and she gets the wrong end of the stick half the time, when I thought better of it. If Mum and Dad got the idea that somebody had given Fish a tiny little puppy a day or two ago, then nobody was going to connect it with the sheep found dead in our field nearly a week past. And they didn't.

Mum and Dad agreed it was nice for Fish to have a puppy. 'He always seems a lonely sort of lad, somehow,' said Dad.

If Fish had been lonely in the past, he was a lot less lonely from then on. About four days later, Floss followed him to school again, and was allowed to stay. Two days later, she turned up again, and for the next two days. The last time, Miss Davies said Fish must take her straight home, lessons or no lessons; it was getting too much of a good thing. After that, Floss left off getting out of her shed.

The only person I told about the dead sheep was Fish. I felt he ought to know, both to be prepared and also so that he would keep an eye on her. I thought he would either be very upset or very angry, but he wasn't either. He just said casually, 'It wasn't Floss; she would never do a thing like that,'

and nothing I could say would make him see that other people might think differently.

He began to teach her some tricks, and she must have been a very clever dog, the way she picked them up. She learnt to sit up and beg, and to act dead, and to shake hands. Fish never seemed to have any big presents, of toys or of money, even at Christmas, but he was always begging a few pennies off his mum to spend on sweets or ice lollies. He taught Floss a very clever trick with sweet papers. Every time he went down to the village to buy sweets, Floss of course went with him. As soon as he had bought his sweets or lolly, he would go out on the doorstep and deliberately drop his sweet papers on the ground. 'Pick 'em up, Floss,' he'd say, and she would pick them up and put them in the litter bin by the door. Of course, when the rest of us saw her do that, we threw our sweet papers on the ground, and she would pick them up, too, and put them in the bin. It used to tickle the grown-ups when they saw her do that. Pete's father once threw an empty cigarette packet down for her to pick up, but she wasn't having any of that. She sniffed it, and left it where it was.

'Quite right, too, Barney,' said fat Mrs Burns, who ran the shop. 'She knows what's bad for you.' Mrs Burns didn't approve of smoking, though she sold an awful lot of cigarettes. She took a real fancy to Floss, perhaps because she kept her doorstep so nice and tidy, and she and Fish between them taught Floss a new trick. When Fish came down to the shop, he didn't go in himself. He would just say, 'Fetch the paper, Floss,' and Floss would go into the shop and stand in front of the counter on her hind-legs. Mrs Burns would say, 'Paper, Floss?' casual and friendly as though Floss were just one of her regular customers, and pop the newspaper into Floss's mouth. Then Floss would trot out of the shop, with her head in the air, holding the paper and looking as pleased as could be. She would carry it all the way to the Ferns, too, if Fish did not take it from her.

What worried me about all this was that somebody might still turn up and claim her. At first I did not like to mention Floss to any grown-up, but one day I was at Tygwyn when Gary was describing her sweet-paper trick to his father. So I said, 'Do you think somebody might still come and say Floss belongs to him, Mr Thomas?'

Mr Thomas considered the matter. 'No, I shouldn't think so,' he said eventually. 'It must be nearly two months since you reported it, and if anybody wanted her they would have made inquiries by now.' I was glad about that, though Fish and I both knew that he could not legally call her his own until three months had passed. But that did not bother Fish. He had been quite sure from the very start that he was going to

37

keep Floss, and it looked as though he was going to be right.

Mr Thomas's remark about Floss being abandoned reminded me about the licence problem. But Fish, who normally never thought ahead about anything, was ahead of me in this case. The very next day, as we came out of school together, he said, 'I've just got to go to the shop to get a licence for Floss.' The shop was also the village post office.

I stared at him. 'Have you got the money?' I asked.

'Yep,' he said.

'How much?'

'Thirty-seven and a half pence.'

'Are you sure?' I asked.

'I know it's thirty-seven and a half pence,' said Fish unconcernedly. 'I asked Mrs Burns.' I could still hardly believe him. For one thing, that wasn't very much money for a grown-up. I could not understand how people would abandon dogs because they could not afford that much. Even so, it was quite a lot of money for Fish to have saved up, because he never saved anything.

However, he turned into the shop just then, and I waited in the doorway. I wanted to see him get it, but at the same time I did not want to be standing at his elbow if he was proved wrong about the money and had to come out looking foolish.

'Come for a dog licence, then, have you dear?' said Mrs Burns. Fish laid his money upon the counter. Mrs Burns took down a folder from behind the post office counter, tore off a form, wrote something in it and stamped it with a date stamp. Fish watched with his sharp black eyes.

'I wonder you did not send your dog down for it,' said a waiting neighbour jovially. Floss was becoming quite famous.

'There we are then, Jimmy,' said Mrs Burns, handing over the paper. 'All paid up and above board now, is it?' I noticed quite a lot of the grown-ups had taken to calling Fish Jimmy lately. I suppose they felt they could not really call him Fish like we did, and James was a bit stiff. Only his father called him that.

Fish thanked her and folded the licence carefully and was putting it away in his pocket when Mrs Burns added, 'You won't lose it now, will you? You'd best ask your father to put it somewhere safe for you.'

'I won't lose it,' said Fish.

'How did you get the money, Fish?' I asked as we walked up the road.

'Oh, that was easy,' said Fish. 'Mr Thomas gave me ten pence the other day because he said I'd been looking after Floss so well, and Mrs Burns gave me another five pence, and the coal-man gave me something for seeing Floss do her tricks, and I saved the rest, if you count what I begged off Mum.' It did sound easy, put like that. Mr Thomas had never given me money, that I could remember, or Mrs Burns. The coal-man did give me sweets sometimes, I must admit.

I could see that having this licence meant a lot to Fish. He could have waited till the three months were up without anyone minding, but he didn't want to wait. Getting the licence made it seem quite definite that Floss really was his very own dog to keep.

'Does your father know you've got the licence?' I asked.

'I don't expect so,' said Fish. 'But Mum knows. She gave me ten pence.'

I wondered who was boss in Fish's family. In our household it varied, but over a thing like one of us having a pet, it was Mum who would have the last word. It was Mum in most things that concerned us as a family, but when it came to the farm, it was Dad.

The trouble was that Mr Barnes never seemed to have a proper job of his own to take his mind off Fish's doings. He had been unemployed when he first arrived. Then he got a job working at a garage, but he gave it up—so he said—after a fortnight. He had a couple of other jobs after that, but neither lasted a month. He had been off work again at the time we found Floss, but now he had taken a job at a warehouse in the town, and had been at it for six weeks.

'We don't see much of Dad now,' said Fish. He did not sound particularly sorry. 'He's working in the evenings, so he's still in bed when I go to school, and I'm in bed when he comes home. So he doesn't bother much about Floss.'

'What about your mother?' I asked.

'Oh, Mum's all right,' said Fish. 'Floss keeps the kids happy.'

'Is she allowed in the house, then?' I asked.

'Yes,' said Fish. 'Dawn's learnt how to open the chicken-house door, see, and after Mum found her in there two or three times with Floss, sitting in all the muck on the floor, she thought it would be easier to keep Floss in the house. Dad doesn't know about that yet. I don't know what he'd say if he knew.'

Fish had these two little sisters. I had always thought of them just as a couple of babies, and couldn't really tell them apart, and Fish scarcely ever called them by name—just 'the kids'—and they mostly seemed to be scrambling about on the floor, wailing and grubby. But lately I'd noticed one of them stumping about the garden, and even talking a bit, so I suppose she was beginning to become a person. That must be the one Fish called Dawn.

'She's not my real mother,' said Fish suddenly. 'But she's all right. She doesn't bother about me much. Too busy with the kids.'

'Why isn't she your real mother?' I asked.

' 'Cos she isn't,' said Fish. 'Dawn and Tracy belong to her, but I don't.'

I tried to think that one out. 'Is Mr Barnes your father?' I asked.

'Uh-uh,' said Fish. 'Worse luck.'

'What happened to your mother—your own mother, I mean? Is she dead?'

'Not so far as I know,' said Fish. After a pause, he added, 'I think she just went off with someone else.'

I felt thoroughly out of my depth. 'Why?' I asked.

'How should I know?' said Fish. 'I was only about three when it happened. I expect she couldn't stick living with Dad any longer.'

I tried to imagine Mum going off and leaving me and Jean and Dan behind. I couldn't.

'Why didn't your mother take you with her?' I asked. I could not see why Mr Barnes should have kept Fish. He didn't even seem to like him very much.

'Couldn't be bothered, I suppose,' said Fish. He kicked a stone along the road in front of us.

'Who looked after you then?'

'I dunno. Some old lady, I think. I was in a children's home for a while.'

'What was that like?'

'It was all right. Different from home. But I've been living with Dad and this Mum now since I was six—except when Dawn was born soon after, and then Tracy soon after that. I went back to the Home when they was coming. I suppose Mum couldn't look after me those times. Not that she's exactly looked after me much anyway. I don't want her to. She leaves me alone and I leave her alone.'

It all sounded very odd to me, and not at all like our home, or any of the other boys I knew. I didn't quite believe the bit about his own mother just going off like that. It didn't seem possible. I decided she must be dead, and they hadn't liked to tell Fish that.

We had got near the Ferns by now, and Floss was wagging herself all over at the gate, having heard our voices.

'Come on then, Floss,' called Fish, and with one bound she was over the gate and down the lane to meet us.

'I've got your licence, Floss,' he said. 'You're really my dog now.'

Chapter 4

ALTHOUGH everybody paid Fish more attention now he had Floss, he was not really one of our gang. I saw more of him than the others because we were the only ones who walked to school from our direction. I usually called for him on the way down, but we did not always walk back together because I often went round by Tygwyn with Gary, which was longer but meant we could play around together for a bit before tea. At first Fish had trailed along after me, but now he always ran straight off home to let Floss out, apart from the one time he had stopped to get her licence. I had stayed with him that time because Gary and I had been arguing about something, and Gary had gone off in a temper.

It hadn't been about anything very much. I just said to Gary that I wished Tom and Pete would play football with us more often, like they used to do. They had left our school the previous year to go with the other big ones on the school bus to town, but last winter as soon as they had eaten their tea they would be out in the field, and we used to have some grand games together. But this autumn things were different. Whenever I asked Tom or Pete if they would come for a game, they always seemed to have homework, or else said they had a practice with the bigger boys in the village. The thing was, the biggest boys in our village used to play matches on a Saturday against teams from other villages, and this year Tom and Pete were in the team.

That was fair enough. But I began to notice that half the matches talked about never came off; and often when Tom said he couldn't play with us because he had homework, or a practice, I'd go down to the village and see him standing about

with the older boys, just talking in a group. It struck me as a poor way to spend an evening, especially as often a group of the girls were hanging around, shrieking and giggling the way girls seem to when they get older.

When I complained to Gary about Tom and Pete never coming to play with us I thought he would agree with me, because things had been rather dull the last fortnight or so, but he got in quite a fret and said he'd got better things to do than go mooning around after Tom all the time. I said of course I didn't do that, and Gary said yes, I did, and Tom was getting sick of it, and I said I didn't, and Gary said I did. It might have been better if we had fought about it, but Gary and I were so used to fighting for fun, we never really thought of fighting for real, so we just didn't speak for the rest of the school day, and then Gary ran off home across the fields and I went with Fish to get the licence.

We forgot about it all right by the next day, but I also

noticed that quite often in school when I was doing my sums or reading, Gary would be leaning across from the double desk we shared to whisper a joke to Fish. I don't know why it was but Miss Davies was always down on Gary and me like a ton of bricks when we giggled in class, but she never seemed to notice when Gary and Fish were up to something. Actually, Fish began to get much better at his work about this time, but I can't think why.

Then, about a month later, something happened which caused a real old upset. You will remember I mentioned the cross-roads near Tygwyn farm. If you come down the lane from our farm to the cross-roads, the main road runs down to the right into the village, and to the left to the market town about seven miles away. That's the way the school bus goes every day, and all the farmers go in their vans on Fridays to the market. Straight across, the lane, which is really a continuation of our lane, winds away past Tygwyn and down to the brook at the bottom, and then up right over the hill to a little hamlet called Llandewi-fach about five miles away, and then on by a roundabout route to the town. It is not a very busy road in the winter, and used only by the people who live up there and by the regular tradesmen, but in the summer a lot of trippers find their way there. Near the top, there's an unexpected right-hand bend. There had been one or two near-accidents, and not long before, a row of posts had been put on the corner, with red reflectors on the one side and white on the other, so as to warn motorists of the danger. Several people had told Mr Thomas that something ought to be done, and I suppose he had told the council men to do it, because he was a County Councillor and chairman of some committee specially to do with roads.

It was a very short time after this that a young man driving a grocer's van went straight over the edge at that very corner. The van rolled over a couple of times and came to rest against a tree; if the tree had not been in the way the van would have tumbled right away down into the bottom of the valley. The man, who was new to the job and had not travelled that way before, escaped with a cut head and some bad bruises. The inside of the van was a right mess, with paraffin spilled all over the butter and bacon and cigarettes mixed up with broken eggs, and the van itself was a write-off. The local policeman, who was Pete's uncle, went up as soon as he heard about it, to see how it had happened—and the first thing he discovered was that somebody had swapped around the reflector plates on the posts, so that anybody coming from the top would see a couple of red reflector posts away on his right, and before he had time to see the further line of them curving away to his left he would have swung the car violently round to the *right*, so as to keep the red lights on his nearside. At least that is what anyone who did not know the road would do, and though it was unlikely, as I said, that one of the first people to come along afterwards would be a stranger, especially at this time of year, that was exactly what did happen.

Sam Morgan, who was the policeman, was good and mad. So was Mr Thomas, and all the grown-ups in the village were saying what a wicked and stupid thing it was to do. It was, too. I couldn't see myself why anyone should want to do such a thing, and I said so to Gary, but he just looked at me a bit queerly and said nothing.

Most people in the village said it was a trick some boys had played, but they were sure it couldn't be any boys from our village. But Sam Morgan was not so sure. He came down the village the next evening when the usual group of boys were gathered by the bridge, and he told them that he had a pretty good idea who had done the trick with the reflectors.

'I'm not saying I've got proof, mind,' he said. 'But I reckon I could soon get proof if I really tried.' All the boys looked blank and innocent. Fish and Gary and I were there too. I suppose we had thought there might be some interesting talk going on down there that night.

'I don't like getting boys into trouble,' Sam went on. 'So I'm doing nothing about it till tomorrow night, when I'm going up to look at them reflectors to see whether the boys that done it have been up and put them back where they belong. I've wrapped some sacking round them for now, for safety's sake. But if they're not back by tomorrow night, then this time I'm going to make trouble for the ones that did it. And it don't matter *who* they are,' he added, pointedly. At that, he looked steadily at each boy, and it seemed to me that the boys he looked longest at were Pete and Tom. Then he left.

There was a little silence, and then the bigger boys began to joke about it. 'Well, I'm off now, up the hill. Anyone lend me a hammer?' 'Hi, Steve, what's that you've got in your pocket? A screw-driver?' And, 'So that's what you were up to last night.' And a lot more. Fish and Gary and I stood around, keeping pretty quiet. Tom and Pete had not said much,

either, but Tom suddenly turned to us and said, 'Hi, you lot, you should be off home. I've got homework to do. Coming, Pete?' They both left the group, and we followed them up the road.

Pete walked straight on past his own house until we reached the gate about two hundred yards out of the village where the Thomas boys usually cut across the fields to their farm. Here we all hung about, not quite sure what to say.

'Tom,' I said at last, 'was it you done the reflectors?'

'Great detective-constable Jimmy Price,' said Tom. 'How did you guess?' He put on a mocking voice, but I thought he sounded pretty uneasy.

'We both did it,' said Pete. 'It was a bit of a lark.'

I was shocked, honestly. 'What if that man had got killed?' I asked.

'He didn't, see? So shut up,' snapped Tom.

'Oh, come on, Fish,' I said. 'Let's go home.'

'Hang on a minute,' Tom said. 'Maybe you can help.'

'How?' I asked, coldly.

'Shall we go and put them back for you?' Fish asked, all agog, silly idiot. But Tom and Pete just glanced at each other.

'*You* couldn't do it,' said Tom.

'Maybe he could,' said Pete.

'Jimmy could, I should think,' suggested Tom.

'You'd be lucky,' I said. I was feeling pretty huffy still, and anyway I thought they were joking.

'Oh, forget it,' said Tom. He sounded miserable, and I don't think he would have said any more about it, but Pete spoke up then.

'Listen,' he said, 'and I'll explain.' Fish and Gary and I climbed up and sat in a row on the gate. Pete leaned against the gate-post, and Tom stood about on the edge of the road, scuffing the dirt about with his toe.

'We reckon Uncle Sam knows very well it was us,' went on Pete.

'How?' I said, though I agreed. I'd seen that long look he gave them.

'I just don't know,' said Pete. 'Maybe Uncle was at our place when we done it, and so he knows I was out then, and Mum may have let on to him that she didn't know where I was. He does come round to see us sometimes in the evening. Maybe someone saw Tom and me out, and mentioned it to him. I don't know how he knows, but he knows.'

'Or anyway suspects,' said Tom.

'Yeah,' said Pete. 'But the thing is this. I don't think he wants all the village to know it was Tom and me that did it, because I'm his nephew, and Tom's father's got a name to keep up—County Councillor and that.'

'I don't see that makes any difference,' said Tom, but he was just saying that for form's sake. He and Pete had obviously talked about this before. 'I don't care what the village thinks,' he added, 'silly lot of so-and-so's; but if Dad knew it was me, he'd . . . oh, I don't know.'

'Slosh you?' asked Fish, brightly.

'No,' said Gary. 'He'd never.'

'I wouldn't care if he did,' said Tom. 'He'd most probably resign from the council or something. I'd never be able to forget it, and Mum would go on so.'

I hadn't much idea what being a County Councillor meant, or what happened if you resigned, but it sounded serious.

'Well, he's not going to find out, so you needn't worry about that,' said Pete. 'The thing is, Uncle Sam has given us this chance to get off the hook. He doesn't want us to get off scot free, but he doesn't want the whole village to know we've done it, and that's what will happen if he decides to take us to court about it.' I looked up, startled; I had never thought of anything like that happening to any of our gang, but Pete obviously thought this could happen, and he ought to know.

'But,' Pete went on, 'if anyone else in the village thought it was us, and people got talking, well, Uncle Sam would *have* to take notice, just *because* he's my uncle, see?' I could see that. 'And if me, then Tom, too, and if Tom, then me.'

'The thing is,' said Tom, 'that if these reflector plates are to be put back without anyone knowing, then it's got to be done tonight, after everyone's asleep. But you know what it's like in our place just now. Mum's up half the night with my grandmother with her bronchitis and has her door open all night and the light on, and never sleeps a wink all night, so she says. I'd have to go right past her open door down that creaky passage. I'd never do it. And then I've got to get back again.'

'You might be lucky,' I said, hopefully.

'It's not good enough,' said Pete. 'Just now, Mr Thomas is mad about those reflectors, but he doesn't suspect Tom and, fair play, if things go right I don't think Uncle Sam will say anything to him to make him suspect. But if Tom's father catches him trying to sneak out of the house in the middle of the night with a screw-driver in his pocket, then that's the first thing he's going to think of.' He paused a minute, and said, 'Of course, I could go by myself; it's a bit risky because you need one person to stand guard, really, but I could do it, I suppose.'

'Don't be nuts,' said Tom. 'If it's difficult for me to get out of our house unnoticed, what about you? Your house is bang slap in the middle of the village, and whichever way you go you've got to walk straight along the village street, with the lights on and goodness knows who looking out of their bedroom window, let alone your Uncle Copper out on the prowl, and not a hedge or a tree to hide behind.'

'I'll go,' said Fish. 'I'm not scared.'

'We couldn't let you go by yourself,' said Tom, quickly. Dang it, I bet they'd let *me* go by myself if I'd offered. They just didn't trust Fish to do the job properly, and nor would I. I said nothing, though, and after a moment Fish said,

'I wouldn't mind. Really I wouldn't. I could take Floss with me.'

All this time, Floss was sitting quietly at our feet, leaning against the gate.

'No,' said Tom. 'Somebody must go with you, or else we must go ourselves.'

I sat on the gate in the darkness saying all the swear words I knew to myself, but I kept my mouth shut. I knew the others were waiting for me to speak. Gary couldn't go any more than Tom; they slept in the same bedroom anyway. There wasn't anybody else to go; only me.

'Look,' I said at last. 'I've got further to go to get to that place than any of you. What happens if I get caught climbing out of our place? Or if we're seen making off up the Llandewi road in the middle of the night? Why should I be blamed for doing such a damned stupid idiotic dangerous thing that even a kid of two would have more sense than to go and do?'

'Scaredy,' said Gary, but the other two said nothing.

'You're a fine one to speak,' I snapped. But I *was* scared, and that was what made me so angry. Fish would be scared, too, if he wasn't such a fool.

But it was Fish who persuaded me. 'Look,' he said. 'They're in dead trouble. Can't you see that? We've got to help.' I was sure he hadn't worked out the first detail of how to set about it, and that it would be left to me to plan everything, and probably to do the job as well, but in this one matter of deciding whether we should go, he was absolutely sure of himself.

'All right,' I said. 'I'll go.'

'Thanks,' said Tom. 'I knew you would.' Oh, yeah? I thought.

'We'd better make some sort of plan, then,' said Pete.

'What for?' I asked. 'I know what to do.'

'Well, for one thing, you must take proper tools with you. You'll need a screw-driver, because they're screwed on. Can you get one?'

'Yes.'

'What about a torch? You'll need a torch.'

'Of course,' I said. I always keep one in my bedroom.

'I've got a torch,' said Fish. 'A little one.'

'A little one's best,' said Tom. 'It's not so likely to give you away. You won't go flashing them around all over the place, will you?'

'We're not all stupid,' I said.

'What's the matter with you, Jimmy?' said Gary. 'I wish I was going.'

'Huh!' I said. 'We'll talk about that another time.'

Tom and Pete were too concerned about the success of the scheme to worry about my remarks. The truth of what Fish had said—'They're in dead trouble'—struck me when I saw that nothing I said, as a cheeky ten-year-old, got a rise out of them.

'You needn't worry,' I said, not quite so snooty. 'We'll fix it now as we go home.' I got off the gate, and so did Fish.

'O.K.,' said Tom, but he was still anxious. 'You won't try and go through the village, will you?'

'And one of you keep watch while the other does the job,' said Pete.

'The only people going over up there will be in cars, and we'll see the headlights,' I said.

Pete hesitated a minute. 'You'd best keep a look-out just in case,' he said.

'We'll take Floss,' said Fish.

'Is that wise?' asked Tom.

'Of course she'll come with us,' said Fish. 'She might howl the place down if I left her behind.' I didn't believe for one moment that she would, but I did not say so. I had a feeling I'd be glad of Floss up there on the shadowy mountain-side. I don't think Tom and Pete felt too happy about the idea of Floss going with us, but they could not risk putting Fish off. We started to move homewards.

'Goodnight,' said Tom. It was a silly thing to say, in the circumstances.

'Sleep well,' I said, sarcastically.

'Look, Jim,' said Tom. 'I am grateful, really I am. We'll have some good games of football after this is over, shall we?'

'Maybe,' I said. And I walked off up the dark road with Fish.

Chapter 5

THERE was not very much to discuss. It was arranged that we would both slip out at twelve o'clock, or as soon after that as was safe. Fish had no watch but he said they had a striking clock downstairs and he could hear that from his bedroom. As soon as he heard it he would get up and dress and then climb out of his bedroom window on to the roof of the lean-to shed below, and from there it was quite easy to reach the old wooden water-butt and so to the ground. He said that was much safer than trying to get downstairs unheard and unlock the door.

I wished I could get out of our house like that. Climbing out of the window was much more adventurous than just walking out of the back door, and discussing plans with Fish was beginning to make me feel it really *was* rather an adventure. After all, we were not planning to do anything wrong—just the contrary, in fact. We were helping our friends *and* making a dangerous bend safe for motorists. I began to wish I hadn't shown myself so reluctant to get mixed up in the business. I suppose the truth is I *am* rather cautious, perhaps because I'm the eldest.

But after all, I told myself, if it all came out, Mum and Dad would *understand*—and I suddenly felt a flash of admiration for Fish, plunging so eagerly into the fray. I would not like to be in his shoes if Mr Barnes found out. And yet, in another way, Fish had little to lose. His father couldn't think much less of him than he did already.

'How will you manage?' asked Fish.

It was almost disappointingly easy for me. I slept in a boxy little room which opened off from the staircase about three

steps from the top. I was not even on the same floor as the others, so all I had to do was creep out and down the rest of the stairs, and out through the dairy door which was never locked. That was at the side of the house, so I could slip off down the lane without crossing the yard, which might wake the dogs. I arranged with Fish that I would walk down the lane towards the Ferns, but if he got out before I was there he would come up to the Rhos.

By this time we were at the Ferns. I don't usually mind going up our lane on my own in the dark, because I am so used to it, but that night I felt suddenly lonely after Fish had disappeared indoors. I jogged home as fast as I could, because the longer I was by myself the less attractive the adventure seemed.

Dan was already in bed by the time I got home, but he wasn't asleep, and he called out I was to come and say goodnight to him. His police hat and truncheon lay on the chair by his bed, and he was sitting up looking wide awake and anxious, like he always looks two minutes before he goes to sleep.

'Tell Jean it's her bed-time,' he said quickly as I went in. He hates the gap between his bed-time and Jean's. Eventually I would sleep with Dan and Jean would have my little bedroom half-way down the stairs, but at present she did not much like the idea of being tucked away from the rest of the family all by herself. That suited me at any time, because of Dan; but tonight it suited me most of all.

'What are you going to do with your truncheon in the night?' I said to Dan, to distract him.

He cheered up. 'If I hear any robbers in the night, I'll get up very quietly and creep down the passage, and I'll creep down the stairs and creep up behind them and then—bash!—I'll clonk them on the head.' That may have cheered Dan up, but it wasn't a very cheering thought for me.

'Goodnight,' I said hastily. 'I'll tell Jean. I expect she'll be up soon.' And I went downstairs, where supper was ready.

There was a television programme I particularly liked after supper, and though I could not concentrate on it tonight, I was glad to have the excuse to stay up later than usual. It was ten o'clock before I was actually tucked up in bed with the light off.

Even so, that left two hours to lie awake before I could go. On the one hand I did not want to let myself get too worked up about it, in case I took fright; on the other, I was afraid of dropping off to sleep. I tried to concentrate on making lists of what I had to do. There was the torch. Yes, that was by my bed. My watch. That was by my bed, too. I decided to put it on now—it would be one less thing to remember when the time came to go. The screw-driver—that was in my anorak pocket. I had collected it from the shed on my way in.

I thought about the job itself. I visualized the shape of the road in my mind, and worked out where it would be best to position Fish as look-out, and found that when I really wanted to picture it in every detail, I couldn't remember the set-up nearly as well as I had thought. It worried me terribly that I couldn't be sure whether there was a straggly hedge on the other side of the road, or just a few windswept stunted trees, and how much of the upper road one could see when working at the top post—or even how many posts there were, or how far apart. . . . Suddenly every bit of me jumped in the bed, like it does just when one is going off to sleep.

That would never do. I looked at my watch, and it was nearly eleven. A scutter of rain beat unexpectedly upon the window. Rain. I hadn't thought of that. I listened, waiting for it to stop. It did for a bit, then it started again. I could hear Mum and Dad going up to bed. That was one thing to be thankful for, at least. I faced away from the door and closed my eyes, breathing slowly and evenly, because Mum usually looked in on her way up.

She paused at the door, which was ajar, said 'All right, Jim?' like she usually did, loud enough for me to hear if I was awake, but soft so as not to wake me up if I was asleep, and then shut the door and went on up the stairs to bed. I'd been anxious before in case she should notice anything, or discover I wasn't asleep, but as soon as I heard the door shut I wanted to jump out of bed and run and open it and tell her I was awake, so that she would come and sit by my bed and talk to me. I knew that was daft, but the tears started running down my face. Then a sob came, and that frightened me so much in case Mum should hear me and come back to find out what was the matter that I forgot about crying and feeling lonely. Instead I felt all coiled up tight with excitement; it would soon be time to go, and it would be the most daring thing I had ever done in my life. I listened; the rain had stopped. The house was silent now; I knew that ten minutes after Mum and Dad had gone to bed, they would be asleep. Life on a farm makes you like that. I looked at my watch again. Eleven-twenty.

Supposing Fish had fallen asleep? Would I have to climb up on that water-butt and across the lean-to roof, and supposing I shone my torch through the window and saw Fish asleep, how would I wake him, if the window was shut? If I tapped on the window, it might wake his parents up first, or set Floss barking. The thought of being found by Mr Barnes squatting on the roof of his house in the middle of the night made me turn cold. Then another thought struck me. What if Fish got the time wrong, and was even now approaching the Rhos, and would start messing about trying to get into my bedroom? I did not trust Fish not to rouse the whole household. Supposing I had made a mistake last time I looked at my watch and it had been twelve-twenty, not eleven-twenty?

I looked at my watch again, and it was all right—twenty-five to twelve now. I decided to start getting dressed, even if it was a bit early. I would rather wait in the lane than have Fish crashing about our ears.

It took longer to dress than I thought, because of trying to be quiet about it. When at last I'd got everything on—jeans, socks, old sweater, old working anorak, not my school one, balaclava helmet—I suddenly imagined Mum appearing at the top of the stairs as I came out of my bedroom fully clothed. Perhaps I should put a dressing-gown on, and look as though I was just going to the toilet. So I crept back and put on my dressing-gown, and at once realized that of course she would see my anorak underneath. Perhaps I could pretend to be sleep-walking, and that I had got dressed in my sleep. But in that case I would hardly put a dressing-gown on top of my ordinary out-door clothes. That only made things look more suspicious. So I crept back and hung it up. I started to the door again, and was just turning the handle when I became

57

conscious of the lump that was the screw-driver in my pocket. If ever anything gave the show away, that did. I was stupid not to have hidden it somewhere out by the lane where I could have picked it up in passing. Should I drop it out of the window, and go round and collect it?

I crept back to the window, and peered out of the little slit at the top of the sash. It wasn't enough to see through, so I tried to edge it down further without making a noise. At first it wouldn't go, then it slid down suddenly with a terrible screech. I stood frozen, waiting for the slightest noise to make me jump straight into bed, clothes and all; but the only sound was my heart pumping.

After a while I relaxed, and leaned out over the window to look down into the yard below. I decided it would be silly to chuck the screw-driver down after all. For one thing it would make a noise and for another it might break on the flagstones, and then where would we be? Then came the problem of shutting the window up again. If it rained any more, it would beat in all over the floor, the way the window was; Mum would know it hadn't been wide like that last thing at night, and she would wonder what I had been playing at. Still, better that than risk another squawk.

I got to the door, opened it quietly and crept downstairs. Out in the dairy, I put on my torch, found my boots and looked at my watch. Where the time had gone to I do not know, but it was already a quarter past twelve!

Ten yards down the lane, something brushed against my legs in the darkness. I stiffened, my heart in my mouth, but it was only Floss. Just behind her came Fish.

'Fish!' I whispered. 'Is that you?'

'What happened to you?' asked Fish. 'Did you fall asleep?'

'I'll tell you later,' I muttered. 'Have you been waiting?'

'No,' said Fish. 'We'd just got here—and now we've got to go all the way down again.' He did not seem bothered. In fact he sounded most cheerful; my spirits rose.

'Come on,' I said. 'This is going to be fun.'

Everything seemed suddenly marvellous. Here we were, out on our own on a splendid adventure in the middle of the night. Everybody else was asleep—Mum and Dad and Jean and Dan, and all Fish's family, and poor Tom and Pete and Gary—and nobody but us knew we were here, setting out on a six-mile walk with a job to be done, and two supermen and a super-dog to do it. We could have laughed and sang, the happiness bubbled in us so, as we ran down the lane, past the Ferns—softly there, but it was velvet dark and there was no danger of our being seen even if Mr Barnes had been leaning out of his bedroom window instead of snoring in his bed. Or at least Fish said he had heard him snoring as he climbed out of his window.

When we got to the cross-roads we could hear a distant car, and saw a broad beam of light approaching from the direction of the village. We huddled back into the deep hedge of our little lane, hugging Floss who thought it was a game and squirmed in our arms, licking our faces, but we were quite safe. The headlights did not pierce the gloom of our turning, and the car swooped by.

After that, we felt pretty safe. It was unlikely a car would use the lane that led past the Thomas's farm and up the hill to the bend and we were sure that if it did, the approaching headlights would give us ample warning. So we skipped along, gay enough and without a care in the world until we did hear a distant car, and saw the lights slanting down the hill. It happened just before another lane joined ours, coming in from the right. This was a short cut from the village, quicker than going up to the cross-roads and down past Tygwyn. The car we could hear was coming down from the famous bend; what we didn't know was whether it would come straight on past us, or swing left into the village.

'Quick!' I said. 'We must hide!' It was only then that we realized it was not nearly as easy as we had thought to take cover in a quiet lane between deep hedges. The hedges on both sides were too high to climb quickly over, too thick to scramble through, and there was no ditch worth speaking of to lie in. The nearest gate was a long way back, unless we ran forward to one that was right on the junction. Then there was Floss, sitting smiling in the road with her tongue hanging out. The question was, which way would the car go?

We took a chance, and stayed right where we were, flattened against the hedge, with our backs to the road. If the car had come our way, it was a hopeless position—we'd have merely looked suspicious without being hidden. But the car went the other way, and we breathed again.

We had learnt our lesson, though. We ran past the junction and down to the little bridge, and as soon as we were over the brook we climbed the rickety stile on the left of the road, and walked by the fields. We kept close alongside the road, at first with a hedge to protect us. But later it was just a wire fence and eventually after the road had gone over a cattle grid, there was nothing to divide it from the bare mountain-side. However, the ground fell away steeply from the road on our side, so all we had to do if anything came along was lie flat on our faces and we would not be seen. It was much harder walking, though. For one thing it was all on a sideways slope, which is all right in the day-time, but tricky in the dark, especially when the ground is hillocky as well, and with patches of uncut thistles, and coils of forgotten fencing-wire in unexpected places. At first, too, we had to keep climbing hedges, and once we stumbled into a flock of sleeping sheep, who set up a great baa-ing. We switched on our torches to help us out of a tight spot from time to time, but we were scared to use them really, because a couple of moving lights up among the sheep would look suspicious to a farmer down in the valley roused by the bleating to look out of his bedroom window.

Fish talked all the time at first, quietly but full of excitement, but then he fell silent, and dropped further and further behind. I did not blame him, because it was tough going, and apart from being bigger than him, I am much more used to clambering about the hills. A month or so ago Fish would never have managed at all, but he had been taking a lot more exercise since he had Floss, and he was keeping up as well as I had expected. I waited for him two or three times but as soon as he caught me up I was urging him on again, because I was getting worried about the time. It had taken longer than we thought to get up there, and I did not know how long it would take to swap the plates around. After that we still had to get home. I think Fish must have felt the same as I did, because he struggled on manfully, although his breath was coming in gasps.

'Is it much further?' he would pant every time he caught me up, and I would say, 'I hope not.'

I kept looking up at the dim line of the road winding round the hill above us, on the look-out for a glimmer of light from the reflectors. I was getting more and more worried because I could not see them, when a tree loomed up on top of us. I switched on my torch to find our way round it, and saw the trunk all scarred and newly-torn, and the ground beneath it churned-up and muddy.

'Hey!' said Fish. 'Isn't that the tree?' Of course it was—the tree that saved the van from rolling down into the valley below. The wreck had been towed away now, and we could see the red grooves cut into the turf by the hawsers that had been used to haul the van up on to the road. We followed the lines up and almost fell over one of the reflector posts in the darkness. All the time I had been looking out for them I had forgotten that Sam Morgan had said he had covered them up with sacking, so no wonder we could not see them from a distance. If we had not run into the tree, we might have slogged right on up to the top without realizing where we had got to.

'Hurrah!' exclaimed Fish. I felt just like that, too. Fish flopped on to the roadside, and I rested there a moment as well, then switched on my torch and went to find the other posts.

There were seven in all, and the one we had found was the third from the top. I pulled the sacking off the top one and examined the plates. They were fastened on with four screws, one at each corner, and not done up very tight because Pete and Tom must have been working in a hurry, and were not trying to make a permanent job of it. It did not look a very long or difficult job, and my spirits rose again.

I got out my screw-driver. 'You keep a look-out,' I called to Fish, and started work.

I soon found it was not as easy as it looked. First I held the torch with my left hand, and the screw-driver with my right. But the screw-driver kept slipping without my left hand to steady it, and when I tried to hold the torch and steady the screw-driver at the same time, the torch just shone straight up into my eyes and dazzled me. I tried propping it on the ground so that the beam would fall on the spot where I was working, but either it kept rolling sideways, or my hands got in the light and I couldn't see anyway. Finally I put the torch out and tried to do it in the dark, by feel. I got on better that way, but when I was on the second screw it came loose before I expected it, and dropped down somewhere in the grass. I patted around with my hands, but I could not feel it any-where, so I put the torch on again and started searching.

You would not believe how long it took me to find it.

'Is anything the matter?' called Fish under his breath. I told him I'd dropped the something screw and he came scrambling up to help me look for it. It was Fish who found it in the end, right down the crack where the concrete base was sunk in the grass.

'Shall I help?' asked Fish.

'No, better not,' I said. 'You go on keeping a look-out.' It was eerie up there; the wind made strange little rustling noises from time to time, and, squatting still doing this fiddly job after all that pounding uphill, I felt cold. Fish began to jump about in the road, swinging his arms to keep warm.

'Hush!' I said irritably. 'Someone will hear you.'

'Who?' asked Fish. He was right, but I was getting fussed by the tiresomeness of the job.

'Go down round the bend and make sure the coast is clear that way,' I said, more to give him something to do than anything else.

Fish and Floss disappeared silently into the blackness, and I persevered with the screws. I got the red plate off, and then, at last, the white one. Now for putting them back again.

At once I realized I must have Fish's help here, because I needed one hand to put the plate up, one to hold the torch to see that the holes in the plate were lined up with the screw-holes in the post, one to fix the screws in and one to hold the screw-driver.

'Hey, Fish!' I called as loud as I dared.

'Here,' whispered a voice at my elbow. 'What do you want?' I explained, but I was disturbed to find Fish could have crept up so quietly on me without my knowing it. It made me feel more edgy than ever.

However, it was much easier to get on with the job with two of us, and having got used to working with Fish holding the light for me, I fumbled hopelessly when I told Fish to put it down and go and keep watch again.

'There's really no need,' said Fish. 'We've got Floss.' So he came and held the torch all the time, and passed me screws when I dropped them. He was pretty good at finding screws in the grass, and he even found a couple that Tom and Pete must have dropped, because there were some missing in places. We couldn't find all the missing ones, but we were able to make sure there were at least three on each plate. We reckoned that was good enough.

'One thing puzzles me,' said Fish. 'About Sam Morgan.'

'And me,' I said. 'How did he mean Tom and Pete to do this job? Like this?'

'It was something else that worries me,' said Fish.

'What?' I asked.

'Supposing he really didn't know who did it, and he thought

63

of a way to find out? He'd think, if I make this plan, the ones that have done it will creep out in the middle of the night and go up there to put them back; then all he'd have to do would be to creep up there himself and catch them at it, and he'd *know* who'd done it.'

'Except he'd be wrong,' I said, but I glanced fearfully round, half-expecting to see a grim caped figure towering over me.

But the only sound was Floss, sitting in the middle of the road biting old burrs out of her shaggy hindquarters.

'I'm glad we brought Floss,' I added.

'So am I,' said Fish.

I remembered Pete hesitating when I had said the only people about would be in cars. Had the same idea that had struck Fish crossed his mind? I wondered about that.

We moved on down to the next post, which was the fifth. It seemed to be taking an awful long time. It wasn't so much that each screw was hard work, but there were four screws on every plate, and two plates on every post, and seven posts, and we not only had to take each plate off, we had to put them back on again. Once I got so muddled I had three-quarters put a red plate back on the same side as I had taken it from before Fish pointed it out. When my fingers got really stiff and cold we swapped jobs, but that didn't work. Fish was too excitable, and *kept* dropping screws, and I was no good at finding them, so we soon went back to doing it the first way. Another tiresome job was getting the sacking off. We had not thought to bring scissors and though I had a pocket knife it was too blunt to be much use. The strips of sacking were all frayed at the edges, and they were sodden wet, and we got all tied up trying to unwind them with numbed fingers. I was already beginning to hate Tom and Pete for their persistence with all those screws, and now I began to hate Sam Morgan too; it wasn't just the sacking, it was the niggling doubt that Fish had left in my mind. Supposing Sam really was on the prowl?

64

We were just finishing the last plate when Floss suddenly gave a low growl. She began to walk, very cautious and stiff-legged, down the road.

'Put your torch out,' I breathed. We held our breath, listening. At first we could hear nothing but the occasional uneasy growl from Floss. Then, without a doubt, we heard measured steps, and at the same instant, Floss broke into a flurry of deafening barks and tore off down the road.

'Floss!' shouted Fish, but I put my hand over his mouth.

'Ssh!' I said, fiercely. Luckily Floss was making such a din no one could have heard him. He realized at once that it was useless to shout for Floss at this stage, and silently we both slithered down the bank. When we were about twenty yards below the road we stopped and listened. The steps were faster now, and a light appeared, bobbing up and down, now and again falling on Floss, leaping around with tail wagging. There was no malice in Floss.

'When he gets up to the bend, and sees we're nowhere on the road, he'll shine his torch down here,' I whispered. 'We've got to get away.' We began to slide on down the hill on our tummies, but then we realized speed was more important than silence. We turned and ran for it, heads down, stumbling over anthills and gorse-bushes in the darkness, until we plunged head-first into the edge of a patch of bracken.

It was a perfect hiding-place. We turned and faced up the hill, lying flat beneath the dank brown fronds, as dank and brown ourselves as any rain-soaked late autumn fern. The shaft of light from the policeman's torch shone up the road, lighting each post in turn. He must have seen the job was done—but if he looked carefully he would see that only two screws held the bottom one in place. But for that, and for Floss's presence, the job could have been finished hours ago, for all he knew.

There was little doubt he would recognize Floss. She was a familiar and popular figure in the village. Would he deduce from her presence that Fish and I were the culprits, and that we were still around? Or would he just wonder? The beam of light left the road and began to travel methodically across the slope upon which we lay, stopping every now and then as it fell upon a hillock or clump of gorse. I did not think it would reach as far as our hiding-place, nor pierce the covering bracken if it did, yet it was an eerie feeling watching it coming our way.

'It's like the telly,' muttered Fish under his breath. 'Cops and robbers.' I knew what he meant. It made me think, too, of the hare I had once come upon, crouched in the corner of a field, with starting eyes and heaving flanks, when I had gone out with the beagles and had left the whooping followers to take a short cut I knew about.

The light was almost pointing directly at us now, and I suddenly felt the urge to stand up and shout 'Pax!' I was not enjoying the game any more, and I wanted to stop it, and play something else.

After all, Sam Morgan was no enemy. He had known me all my life and taught me my kerb drill in the infants' class, and trained me for my cycling proficiency test last year. He was Father Christmas at all the village parties and he was a great

favourite of Dan's, whom he always referred to as his 'colleague'. What had I done wrong that I should be cowering away like this?

On the other hand, it *was* a thrilling game, and we were on the winning side. Why give in now? I glanced at Fish lying tense beside me, and realized there was no question of 'Pax'. He was having the time of his life, no doubt about that. But that wasn't the point. If we came forward, Sam would probably believe our story, but he would want to take the matter to our fathers.

I could face that, in my family. It would be unpleasant, but no more so than the continued deception. It would be like choosing to have a tooth out instead of putting up with the ache. But what about Fish?

Fish nudged me. 'Look!' he said. Floss, having got over her excitement about meeting the policeman, had realized that we were no longer around, and was sniffing along the grass verge where we had rolled away down the hill, to see where we had got to. Sam stood watching her with great interest. He knew what she was thinking about as well as we did.

'Attaboy!' we heard him say, encouragingly. 'Hi lost, then! Hi seek! Good dog!' That was a mistake from his point of view. The words meant nothing to Floss, but she was delighted to be spoken to, and she left off looking for us, and proceeded to jump up him.

'Down, dog!' he said. 'Down!' Floss got down, and looked at him hopefully. 'Go on, then! Hi seek! Find your master! Seek him out! Seek him out!' Floss did her very best to please. In the light of the torch we could see her wriggling around Sam in circles, not liking to jump up again, wagging her tail to show her pleasure, cringing because she wanted to do the right thing but she could not make out what it was. It was a good thing Sam was an even-tempered sort of bloke. 'You're bloomin' useless, you are,' we could hear him say in a resigned sort of voice, and we rolled on the grass in our hide-out in helpless giggles, clutching each other.

Then Sam turned his attention to the upper slope on the other side of the road. The ground rose steeply on that side, and then levelled off. Sam could not see much from where he stood, but he decided that if he climbed up the steep bank he would get a good view over the open hillside, and this he proceeded to do. His back was turned to us, and his torch was pointed in the opposite direction. Floss was not visible with him, so we guessed she had stayed down on the road, and we could picture her standing alert, wondering where we had got to.

'Shall I whistle?' said Fish.

'Try,' I answered, '—not too loud.' Fish's first attempt would not have awakened a beetle asleep under his nose. 'A bit louder than *that*,' I said. Fish tried again. The light went jigging steadily on uphill, so we knew Sam had heard nothing. But had Floss? We waited in the dank darkness, and Fish was just beginning another little flute when suddenly Floss was upon us, all long wet hair and long wet tongue.

We crawled away under the canopy of bracken, turning now and again to keep that bobbing pinprick of light in view. Then, suddenly as we moved, a nearer horizon rose blackly against the skyline and blotted out the light. We had got under the lee of the curve of the hill, and were safe.

We broke cover and ran on down to the bottom of the valley. From here we could follow a brook straight down to where it joined the main stream, the only difficulty being the number of hedges and fences we had to cross and the fact that it ran past Aberdulais Farm. Williams's place, that was, the man who owned the sheep we had disturbed on the way up. We got past safely, though, without having to go close enough to risk waking the farm dogs; Floss followed at our heels as if she did this sort of thing every night of her life. Or at least she did until we met the hare.

It happened just after we had reached the main brook and were making our way quietly upstream towards the bridge. The question was, whether we dared get back on the road in order to cross by the bridge or whether we ought to wade across, in case Sam had come down again and was waiting there. I shone my torch upon the water; it looked full and fast and deep. At the same time I glanced at my watch, and saw it was already four o'clock. My father was sometimes up by five. I felt fagged out, and I was sure Fish was even more so.

'Come on. We'll go by the bridge,' I said. But we stopped under cover of the hedge by the rickety stile to peer into the gloom in case a dark figure was lurking there. We were so still that the old jack hare, going about his business, almost hopped into us before he saw us, or we him. Then I saw his eyes staring at me, barely a yard away. 'Look,' I breathed, putting a hand on Fish's knee, but the movement gave us away. With a jerk and thud of the powerful hind legs the hare went scudding up the slope, dodging and turning but always seeking the higher ground. And after him, like a streak, went Floss.

Fish had the sense not to shout after her this time, and the fact that the sudden commotion had caused no movement on the road showed us that the coast was clear.

'Let's go,' said Fish. 'She'll catch us up.'

We nipped over the stile, across the bridge and straight on up the road until we came to the first gate beyond the short cut to the village. Perhaps it was risky, but we were getting too tired to care. From there we only had one field to walk across to come out by the cross-roads—positively no more hedges to climb. There was still no Floss, but Fish was not bothered. 'She knows her way home from there,' he said.

'What happens if she doesn't catch us up before we get back?' I asked.

'I'll have to go down and let her in,' said Fish. 'I had to do that a few nights ago, when she got out somehow. Dad caught me at it so if he finds me doing it again he won't think much about it.'

'Was he cross?' I asked.

'Only because I had woken him up,' murmured Fish. He

kept yawning and sounded so drowsy he could scarcely put the words together.

'He'll think more about it if he catches you looking like that,' I remarked, but Fish did not hear me. We were at the gate on to the cross-roads, and while I opened it Fish walked through like someone in a dream. I turned to shut it and heard Fish mutter something that sounded like 'I'm so sleepy'. When I turned back again he had crumpled gently on to the grass verge of the main road and was fast asleep!

'Fish!' I exclaimed. 'Fish! Wake up! You can't sleep here!' It was ridiculous. After all our adventures and escapes, Fish had chosen here, of all places, to settle down for his night's sleep. I shook him and punched him, and hauled him to his feet. What if a car should come along now? It wasn't likely, at four-fifteen in the morning, but it could happen.

'Wassa mather?' asked Fish drowsily, as I heaved him across and into our lane.

'Fish!' I said fiercely. 'You must wake up!'

'Mm?' said Fish. Then he seemed to pull himself together. 'Did I fall asleep?' he asked, in surprise.

I could not be cross with him, but I was terrified that he would fall asleep again before he got back to the Ferns. It wasn't far, but it seemed a very long way that night.

At last we were there.

'I'm coming round the back with you,' I said.

''S'no need,' murmured Fish. But I went with him, and helped him up on to the water-butt.

'Hey!' I whispered. 'What about your boots?' He was preparing to climb back into his bedroom complete in his filthy wellingtons. The rest of his clothes were not exactly spotless, but maybe he could hide them for a time.

'Oh, yes,' he said. He kicked them off down to me from the lean-to roof. 'Put them in the chicken house, where Floss sleeps.' There was still no Floss.

'Could I leave the door open for her?' I asked.

'Good idea,' said Fish. 'It will look like an accident if

72

anyone notices.' I couldn't see Fish being awakened by a little whine from Floss to go down and let her in. I didn't think if she could trumpet like an elephant it would rouse him.

'Don't forget to get undressed and hide your muddy clothes,' I whispered. I was talking to him as though he were Dan.

'I'm not stupid,' he said, looking down at me with one leg over the window-sill. I could sense he was grinning, sleepily.

'Only sometimes,' I said, grinning back. We had done it, hadn't we? It was nice to feel joky and friendly with Fish.

I stepped carefully off the water-butt, put Fish's boots in the chicken house, leaving the door ajar, and crept back out on to the lane again. Then I stumbled off up our track, hoping I would not fall asleep in the ditch, like Fish.

I got home without further incident, let myself quietly in and crept up the stairs to bed. It took a tremendous effort of will to get undressed and stow my clothes away under the bed, but I managed it. I even thought to wipe my face with a wet flannel, because I had a kind of a feeling I might be asleep when Mum called to say it was time to get up. I looked at my watch as I got into bed, and it said five o'clock.

For all I know, Dad may have started getting up two minutes after I got into bed.

Chapter 6

THREE hours later I swam up from fathoms deep, hauled to the surface by the tug of insistent voices calling.

'Are you *coming*, Jimmy?' It was my mother's voice, and from her tone it was not the first time she had shouted up to me.

The part of me that talks managed to say, 'Just coming, Mum,' before burrowing back under the waves to join the rest of me.

But it was no good. It may have been ten minutes later, but it seemed like the same instant, I could feel my mother's hand on my shoulder, shaking me.

'What's the matter with you, Jimmy? Are you all right?' she said.

I yawned and rolled round to look at her. 'I'm all right,' I said. 'Just sleepy.'

'It's twenty past eight,' she said. 'I'll go and tell Jean to start on down with Dan. They'll miss the car, else. Now, don't you go back to sleep as soon as I've gone,' she added, turning round from the door. I sat up hastily, still keeping my hands under the bed-clothes. I did not want her to strip me as there might be a fair amount of mud in the bed.

Luckily she went down then, and I got up and washed. I also made my bed, which I did when I felt good, but Mum would probably think I was mad to do it when I was already so late.

Mum looked at me suspiciously when I got downstairs. 'Are you sure you're feeling all right?' she asked.

'Quite,' I said. 'I woke up in the night, that's all, and couldn't get to sleep again until nearly morning.' That was

74

true enough. 'Can I have another slice of bread and jam?' If Mum was still worried she must have been reassured by the size of breakfast I ate. I was ravenous.

'You can't stop and eat any more,' she said firmly at last. 'You must *go*. You'll have to run all the way as it is.' As I scrambled into my school anorak she added, 'If Fish isn't out on the road, don't waste time going to knock on the door. I expect he will have gone on by now.'

He could have, or equally he could still be in bed asleep. His mother was not as persistent as mine. If he was, there did not seem much sense in drawing attention to the fact that we had both overslept, so I did not stop at the house.

Gary was waiting for me anxiously at school, but assembly was just starting, so we could not say much.

'Everything go off all right?' he whispered.

'Yes,' I whispered back, hastily finding the hymn number.

Fish had still not turned up by roll-call, so I decided he probably was not coming. When his name was read out, I said as much, adding that he was not there when I called by.

'That was what made you a bit late, was it, Jimmy?' asked Miss Davies, going on down the list. She did not wait for an answer, and she did not get one. Gary grinned at me meaningfully. I wondered suddenly whether Floss had got home all right, and at what time.

It was not easy to find a quiet moment at school to tell Gary all that had happened, so the full story had to wait until we walked back home together. Then I told him everything, including about Sam Morgan prowling around up there.

'The sly thing!' exclaimed Gary indignantly, when he heard. Then he added, 'It was jolly clever of you not to get caught; I bet Tom and Pete will be pleased.'

As I passed the Ferns Mrs Barnes came to the door, carrying Tracy. Dawn toddled out from behind her and stood looking at me, thumb in mouth.

'Hullo, Jimmy Price,' said Mrs Barnes. 'Looking for our

Jimmy?' I liked the way she said that. 'I thought he must be bad this morning, he was sleeping so heavy. By the time he woke up, it was too late to send him to school, so I let him have a good lie-in. He's up now, though. I think he must be out somewhere with Floss, though I never saw him go—did we, Dawn?'

Dawn took her thumb out of her mouth. 'Floss! Floss!' she lisped and staggered towards the gate, pointing. And there

Floss was, waggling with pleasure at finding me there. Dawn blundered into her as she came in at the gate, and sat down with a thump.

'If Floss is here, our Jimmy won't be far away,' remarked Mrs Barnes, and at that moment Fish appeared. I had never seen him looking so dirty, but then I realized he was wearing the clothes he had got on last night. That was why he had slipped out unnoticed, I thought.

'Good grief!' commented Mrs Barnes, lazily. 'What do you think you've been playing at?'

'I'm sorry,' said Fish. 'I fell in the bog. I didn't mean to.'

He obviously had been in the bog, too; last night's dirt was well hidden under a more recent layer. I thought about the wet bundle at the back of my cupboard, and decided the sooner I went and fell in a bog the better. If Fish had been a little dirty, Mrs Barnes might have been cross, but he was *so* dirty he was funny. Only someone with no sense of humour could have been cross—Mr Barnes, perhaps. Was Mrs Barnes like that, too?

I looked anxiously at her. She had long gold hair, rather straggly and dark at the roots. Dyed, Gary said. She couldn't have felt the cold much because whenever I saw her she had bare plump arms and bare legs, her feet slipped into tatty but gay slippers, and silky knitted jumpers with low necks and no sleeves.

As I watched her, the corners of her mouth twitched. 'Boys!' she remarked briefly. She turned to put Tracy down indoors, but before she shut the door she called over her shoulder, 'You'd better let me have those things to wash before your dad comes home.'

'Everything been O.K.?' I asked Fish.

'Yeah,' said Fish. 'I didn't wake up until dinner-time. Did you get to school?'

'Mum saw to that.'

'My mum don't bother much. It's just as well one of us showed up. What did Gary have to say?' Fish was obviously sorry not to have been there to tell the story. We agreed to meet at ten o'clock the next morning and go down to Tygwyn together to report to Tom.

I was just going when I remembered something.

'I see Floss turned up all right,' I said. 'Did you hear her come in?'

'Not likely,' said Fish. 'I never saw her till dinner-time, but she must have been there first thing, or Mum would have said something. I expect she got home just after we did.' I was starting to walk on when Fish ran a few steps after me.

'It was great last night, wasn't it, Jimmy?' I nodded. He gave me a comical look. 'What about going up there again tonight and putting all them plates on back to front again, eh?'

I laughed. 'You can go by yourself, then. I didn't sleep till dinner-time like some people!' We parted, both feeling very happy.

'I can't wait to get home and fall in a bog!' I shouted back down the lane.

That was my next concern—to get upstairs, put on the dirty wet things I had been wearing last night, get out of the house unobserved and find some really mucky job to do about the farm.

Luck was with me. It was Friday and Mum and Dad had not long been home from market.

'Dad would like you to help him bring down some sheep,' said Mum as I came in, 'so have a bite of tea now before you change, and then go and get into your old clothes. He wants to get up there before dark, but he'll be fetching the cows in first, so just have some bread and butter now—I'll give you something hot for your supper when you come in.'

That suited me, because usually I changed before tea, and that would have been difficult. So I drank off a mug of tea, with plenty of milk in it to cool-it, so that Mum wouldn't think to suggest I left it to cool while I went and changed, sloshed some jam between two thick rounds of bread and butter, and

78

went upstairs munching it. As I pulled on my wet things, flinching a bit at the cold dampness of them, I could hear the cows mooing and squelching in from the back pasture, and Dad talking, soothingly to the cattle, sharply to the two dogs, who were no doubt lively after spending most of the day shut up.

Then I came cautiously down the stairs, made sure Mum was in the kitchen, and instead of going out that way like I usually do, I slipped round the other way through the dairy. 'I'm off, Mum,' I shouted from the door, and shut it quickly in case she thought of something to say to me.

Dusk had fallen, so it was unlikely that Dad would notice the state of my clothes. He was just leaving the milking-shed as I came round the corner.

'Ready?' he said. 'Did your mother tell you I want to get the sheep down from the top field tonight?'

'Yes,' I said, and measured my length in the midden. I could not have done it better if I had tried, and, believe me, I had not tried. I had fully intended to stumble in the strip of marsh above the farm, but I suppose because I had come running round the side of the farm instead of straight out into the yard I had tripped on some unexpected obstacle.

'Hold up!' said Dad, a bit late in the day. Then, as he heaved me up, he added, 'You're in a right pickle. How'd you come to slip?'

'Something rolled under my feet, I think,' I said.

Dad poked about with his foot while I wiped my face.

'Hey,' he said. 'What's this?' He bent down and picked up—Dan's truncheon! I felt foul, all that muck dripping down me, but common sense told me I should be grateful to Dan.

'You'd best go and change again,' said Dad.

'It's only my jeans, really,' I said. 'I shan't be a minute.'

I went boldly in through the kitchen door this time, brandishing Dan's truncheon. Mum was quite sorry for me and when Dan said, 'Pooh! I can smell something,' very pointedly, Mum let him have it.

I was soon fit to go out again—it would have been a waste of time to be too particular—and I jogged up the hill, taking care *not* to fall in the marsh, and soon caught up with my father.

When I got my breath back, I asked him why the sudden rush to get the sheep down. He hadn't said anything about changing their pasture before, and I didn't see why it had to be done on market day.

'There's been dogs after some sheep again,' said Dad.

'Ours?'

'No, no. I heard at the market. Pugh lost two sheep three nights ago, and there was four killed at the farm across the valley last night.' Pugh owned the land next to us, on up the road towards the town.

'Which farm was it last night?'

'Williams, it was, Aberdulais.'

I said nothing for a long, long time. Aberdulais was the farm we had passed through on our adventure. It was on Aberdulais land that we had disturbed the sheep on our way up, and on Aberdulais land that we had met the hare, that had run away up across the slope towards those sheep, with Floss in hot pursuit. And nobody knew what time Floss had got home. I remembered something else—Fish telling me how he had let Floss in another time, about three nights ago. But Floss, with her ridiculous good humour and her endearing tricks—*not Floss*.

I took a deep breath. 'Did anyone see any dogs?' I asked.

'No,' said Dad. 'They're too damn clever, these killer dogs.'

Floss was clever, no one could deny that. *But not in that sort of way.*

We got the sheep down to the home pasture. 'We'll hear them there, if there's any sort of trouble,' said Dad. Later that evening I noticed Dad taking his shot gun up to his bedroom. The window looked out over that field. He caught my anxious look.

'I don't suppose I'll use it,' he said. 'I don't want to, not if

I can help it. But this sheep-killing has got to be stopped. There's others besides us who are going to suffer if those dogs aren't destroyed.'

After I had gone to bed I had an idea. I thought I would slip out again after everyone was asleep, and go down to the Ferns and make sure Floss was safely shut in. Then, if some more sheep were killed that night, I could prove it wasn't Floss. It was quite a good idea; the only trouble was I fell asleep before I had a chance to carry it out. After all, I had only had three hours sleep the night before.

Next morning I called for Fish as arranged and we went on down to Tygwyn. There had been no trouble with our sheep in the night, and Tom and Gary did not seem to have heard of the other incidents Dad had talked about. Pete arrived soon after and we all five went and sat in the barn among the bales of hay, and talked while Floss rooted for mice. It was like old times, only better, because now Fish was one of us, instead of an outsider.

Pete had news for us. His Uncle Sam had called last night and had a long talk with him, admitting that he *had* suspected Pete and Tom, because he had called in, the evening the reflectors were swapped, and nobody knew where Pete had got to, and he did not give a very convincing explanation when he got home about ten o'clock at night. But Sam was not *sure*. So he had said the bit, publicly, about the culprits going back to undo the damage, in order to find out. At the time, he had not intended to go up and catch them at it, but had reckoned that if he went up in the morning and found the job done, then he would know it was boys from our village, and therefore probably Tom and Pete; but if nobody had been near the place, then that pointed to it being the work of boys from somewhere else.

Tom and Gary and Fish and I looked at each other then. That was something we had never thought of. In fact, far from clearing Tom and Pete from suspicion, Fish and I, by our action, had actually brought it upon them.

Not exactly, Pete went on. After talking to the boys, Sam had done a bit more thinking, and he realized that what he had said amounted to *asking* the boys responsible to slip out of their homes in the middle of the night. So he lurked about quietly in the village, keeping a watch on Pete's house, half the night, so that if Peter emerged and joined up with Tom, he could catch them before they ever went up the hill and pack them off home again. He would also know who had done it and could give them a thoroughly good talking-to and really shake them up, without anybody else knowing anything about it, including Tom's parents. By and large, it was quite a decent plan, really.

But of course it did not work out like that. Sam must have got pretty cold and fed up standing around watching Pete's house while all the time Fish and I were making our way up by the other road. At about half past twelve he had stopped a car that had come down off the top, and the driver told him nobody was up there, so he did not think he could have missed them.

That must have been the car that nearly caught us out in the lane by Tygwyn.

Sam was just about to pack it in and go home when he heard a lot of bleating from sheep high up across the valley. That was when we disturbed the Aberdulais sheep on our way up. No doubt the thought of dogs crossed his mind—Dad had reported our loss three months ago, and maybe Mr Pugh had told him about his much more recent one.

Or it could be the culprits on their way to or from the bend. Sam decided to investigate. He cycled until the road got too steep, and then leaned his bike by the cattle-grid and walked quietly on. All he found when he got up there was Floss. We knew that part.

While he was looking around, Floss disappeared, and in due course Sam made his way home, much puzzled. Floss, of course, pointed to Fish being involved, and as Fish was unlikely to go and do a thing like that on his own, his most likely companion would be me or Gary. He knew enough of the Thomas's set-up to discount Gary, which left me.

'And he really did not think it would be you, Jimmy,' said Pete, 'nor Fish either. He said you were too sensible and Fish was too little.'

'Huh!' said Fish.

At that point in his thoughts, Sam decided to visit Pete and bring the whole thing into the open.

'He asked me,' said Pete, 'if I'd been out of the house last night, to put back the reflectors. Or Tom. I said no, what had it got to do with us? That puzzled him. Then he said could Jimmy and Fish have been up the night of the crash, meddling with them? I said no, of course not. Jimmy and Fish had been in their houses at that time, and anybody could prove it. He asked all the wrong questions, see? Then he let on about finding Floss up there, and I said I didn't know nothing about that, but dogs could wander sometimes. I said I thought Floss did get out in the night sometimes, so it wouldn't be the first time. He said it was a long way from her home—but he hadn't anything else to go on, except that the plates were back. Finally he just said he was sorry, and he thought it must have been some older boys, because they'd made a pretty good job of it, and not left anything behind, because he had had a good look.'

Tom grinned at us and gave the thumbs-up sign.

'And he never asked you, straight out, if you were the ones that put them wrong in the first place?' asked Gary.

Pete hesitated a moment, looking uncomfortable. 'Well, yes, he did in the end,' he admitted, 'and I said no. I had to, by then.'

'You couldn't help that,' said Tom. 'We'd have all done the same in your place—except Jimmy, perhaps.' I wasn't quite sure how to take that, so I said nothing. 'It's all over now,' he went on, as he stood up and stretched, 'and we're jolly grateful. What about that game of football?'

It was a great game of football, but the business of the

reflector plates was very far from being all over—as far as
Floss was concerned.

*   *   *

I worried a good deal about how much I should say to Fish
about the sheep-killing, and in the end decided to go on
saying nothing, but to carry out my plan to go and check on
Floss in the night. If I could *prove* she was innocent there
would be no need to upset him.

That night—Saturday night—I managed to stay awake until
after my parents had gone to bed, and then I dressed and
crept downstairs much as I had done two days before. It
seemed much less alarming this time. I started off towards the
Ferns—and half-way down the lane Floss met me.

My heart sank. 'What are you doing here, Floss?' I asked.
She was as friendly and ridiculous as ever, and followed me
eagerly back to the Ferns. She was wet, certainly, but she did

not appear to be panting or tired. When I got there, and went to the door of the chicken run, she drew back reluctantly, and then moved out towards the lane, tail whisking, head on one side. It was moonlight that night, and I could see her perfectly. 'Shall we go for another midnight adventure?' she seemed to be saying.

'No, Floss,' I whispered. 'Come here.' I was afraid Mr Barnes might look out and see me in the clear moonlight. She came obediently enough then, and crept past me into the shed, tail down and looking so dejected I could not help feeling sorry for her. As I fastened the catch I noticed unless you gave the door a good pull it did not slip right home. There was a bar that fitted into a slot on the inside, to fasten the door. You opened the door from the outside by slipping your fingers through a hole specially cut for the purpose and pushing the bar up, but if the door were not pulled tight the bar only just caught on the lip of the slot. A clever dog would be able to push it up with its nose, and swing the door open. Nobody would ever dispute that Floss was a clever dog.

I made sure the door was tight shut, and went home.

*   *   *

At about half past ten next morning, Sam Morgan arrived at our place. I was out in the yard at the time, playing with Dan.

'Hullo, Jimmy,' said Sam, pleasantly enough. 'And how's my colleague getting on these days?' he said to Dan. 'Been making any arrests lately?' Then he asked to see my father.

I took him into the house—the only time you will find Dad sitting down by the fire in the day-time is on a Sunday morning, because he doesn't go to chapel till evening. I was scared rigid in case Sam had found out about the reflectors. It wasn't about that, though, that Sam had come. It was because Mr Thomas had lost three sheep in the night, and Sam wondered if ours were all right.

I went out then, feeling rather sick suddenly, and stood in

the yard, thinking. Three months ago, we'd lost our sheep; that was the day Floss turned up out of nowhere. Earlier this week, Floss had been out in the night, and earlier this week Pugh had lost sheep. On Thursday Floss had disappeared while out with us on the Aberdulais land, and on Thursday night Williams had lost sheep. Last night the Thomases had lost sheep, and only I knew that Floss had been out then. That was four times; and every time sheep had been killed, Floss had been out.

But there was another side to it. Supposing Fish *never* shut the door tight, perhaps on purpose because he found it difficult to open. If that were so, the fact of Floss being out on the nights the sheep were killed would not mean a great deal—except that it was odd those were the only nights I had reason to *know* she was out.

I didn't like the look of it at all, and I decided that the time had come when I must go and see Fish about it.

Sam came out about then, and, giving me a friendly good-bye, stamped off down the lane. I gave him time to get clear, and, asking Dan to tell Mum where I had gone, I went down after him.

Fish was in his so-called garden when I got there, playing with Dawn, much as I had been with Dan. He had seen Sam go up to our place, and naturally wanted to know why, but as soon as I said it was about the sheep, and told him about the killings, Fish lost interest. Then I told him about the dates, and how they always coincided with the nights Floss was out.

'So what?' said Fish. 'You don't think she did it, do you?' He just could not conceive of such a thing being possible. So then I told him about last night, and how I had come down to see if Floss was safely in, and how I met her on the lane. He said nothing for a moment, but then he swung on me with his face flushed with anger, and said,

'You've got a nerve!'

'How do you mean?' I asked, taken aback a bit.

'Snooping around like a blinkin' spy! Going around being all friendly, and pretending you like Floss and everything, and all the time secretly planning to get her accused of killing sheep.'

'Fish,' I said, 'don't be daft. It's not like that at all, really it isn't. I was only trying to help.'

'Help? Don't make me laugh!'

'Honest I was,' I said. I was beginning to get cross myself, but I tried to keep calm.

'I hate you,' Fish suddenly shouted. 'I hate you, hate you, do you understand?'

I bent to stroke Floss, who was rubbing against my legs.

'Don't touch her,' shouted Fish. 'I won't have you touching her. Go on, go on home. Clear off!'

'All right then,' I said. I meant it to sound cool and casual, but I suddenly found I was crying. I turned away and stormed back up our hill, miserable and furious.

The quarrel was important, because it meant Fish and I did not tell each other things in the next couple of days, as we would normally have done. If we had, events might have been very different.

Sam Morgan went home and did some thinking and looked up his police records. He discovered, for example, that Floss turned up the same day as we lost our sheep. He noted that the Aberdulais sheep were killed the same night that he saw Floss, and then lost her again, up on the hill; and he remembered what Pete had told him about Floss being out a few days earlier. Late in the afternoon, he put his notebook in his pocket and went up to see Mr Barnes at the Ferns about the matter.

There were a number of things Mr Barnes was not aware of at this time. He had not realized that three months had now elapsed since Floss had been brought to the Ferns, nor that Fish had got her licence. One or two people had remarked to him that his boy had looked after the dog very well, and had spoken admiringly of her clever tricks. Mr Barnes rather enjoyed this—but that did not mean he felt responsible for her. Sam explained the position.

'Of course I quite see, quite see,' said Mr Barnes. 'Only took the dog in out of kindness, as you know. But it's not our dog, see, not our dog. Boy will have to realize that. You had better take her away with you right away.'

Sam must have seen Fish's stark face in the background. 'We've no proof, mind,' he said carefully. 'No proof at all. It's just that that's the way things are pointing. I thought if I warned you, and you could keep the dog under surveillance—watch her, like, you know—we could see what happens. There's no need to do anything drastic right away.'

That was not at all what Mr Barnes wanted. He did not want to give cause for offence, and anyhow, the dog was not his. It was a police problem.

Here Sam put him right. Mr Barnes was the legal owner of the dog. It had been kept at his house for more than three months, unclaimed, and he had taken out a licence for it.

No, said Mr Barnes, there Mr Morgan was wrong. He had not realized the three months was up, and he would never consider taking out a licence because it had only been a temporary arrangement; if the three months was up, the dog must go.

When Sam quoted the date and serial number of the licence, Mr Barnes began to get confused. Fish obliged the constable by fetching the licence; Mr Barnes was getting very edgy. While Mr Barnes fretted, Fish kept silent and still. Sam turned to him and explained exactly and in detail very much what I had said to him this morning. In fact, it was so much the same that Fish jumped to the conclusion that I had been collaborating with Sam up at the Rhos that morning. But there was one important difference.

'Listen,' said Sam. 'The only time when sheep have been killed and we do not know that Floss was loose was last night. Can you prove that she was safely shut up all last night, because if you can, then we know some other dog was responsible for that killing, and so maybe for all of them?'

'Last night?' said Fish, innocently. 'Oh, yes, I know for sure she was in all last night.' But then he lost his head, and shouted, 'and if Jimmy Price says any different, then he's telling a pack of lies!' And he turned and ran out of the room.

'Oh, dear,' said Sam.

'Can't believe him, just can't believe a word he says,' said Mr Barnes.

Mrs Barnes had come in half-way through the conversation, and was only just beginning to grasp what it was all about, but she turned now and said to her husband,

'Come now, Will, that isn't a nice thing to say about your own son. He's all right, is our Jimmy. He's a good lad, if you'd only let him be.' But the harm had been done.

'Of course,' said Mr Barnes, 'I'll be sorry to lose the dog, but when something's got to be done, there's no use grumbling. The last thing I would wish is to cause any trouble in the neighbourhood, Constable, you can be sure of that.'

'*You'll* be sorry?' said Mrs Barnes. 'What about our Jimmy? Break his heart, he will.'

Mr Barnes seemed genuinely surprised. 'James is only a little boy,' he said. 'He has to learn to do what's right, same as any other child. He'll soon get over it—that's kids all over.'

Mrs Barnes would have answered, but Dawn wailed from upstairs. She had been put to bed with a tummy upset. 'I've been sick!' she howled. Tracy was hanging round her mother's ankles, whimpering to be picked up. With a sigh, Mrs Barnes swept up Tracy and ran upstairs.

In the quiet that ensued, Sam fidgeted. 'I wouldn't be in too much of a hurry if I were you,' he said. 'We'll leave it a bit, shall we?'

'It's kind of you, Constable, I'm sure,' said Mr Barnes, 'but I hope I know my duty. It would be best if you'd take that dog right away now, and have her put down.'

90

But there Sam put his foot down. It was not his respon-
sibility, he said. The dog belonged to Mr Barnes now. No
policeman would go around taking other people's dogs off
them and having them destroyed, without a court order. If
Mr Barnes wished to have the dog put down, then he must
make the appropriate arrangements himself. But if he wanted
to know what Sam thought, then he should not rush into
getting rid of Floss without giving her a further chance to
prove her innocence. And feeling extremely uncomfortable,
Sam went home.

I gathered much of this story from Pete, who heard his
Uncle Sam telling his mother about it, and some came out
when Mrs Barnes came to visit our place in great distress
several days later.

There was no doubt that Mr Barnes was very angry indeed
that night. Not only had he found himself saddled with a dog
that he had never wanted and that had brought him into
disgrace in the neighbourhood—so he fancied—by being
suspected of sheep-killing; but also he had been made to look
a fool in front of the village policeman by his son. What was
more, that son had the audacity to fight every inch of the way
in the struggle to save Floss, and even his wife was inclined to
take sides against him.

Only two things emerged clearly afterwards. One was that
as my father walked home from chapel that night, he heard
Fish screaming and screaming inside the Ferns, and the voice
of Mr Barnes raised in uncontrolled anger. The other was
that Fish was to miss school the next day in order to walk into
town and deliver Floss over to the vet, and that Mr Barnes
would meet Fish outside the place where he worked and bring
him home on the back of his motor-cycle. The reason for this
seemingly heartless plan was simple. When Mr Barnes cooled
down sufficiently to think things out, he simply did not know
how to achieve what he had sworn was to take place. He could
not take Floss into town himself on his motor-cycle and unlike
most local people he did not possess a gun and had no idea

91

how he should set about disposing of a full-grown dog himself.

Mrs Barnes objected strongly.

'If you want the dog dead,' she said, 'you should do your own dirty work and not expect the boy to do it.' She even asked him to leave it a day or two until Dawn was better, and she would ask Mrs Price the Rhos to look after the two little girls while she took Floss in herself. 'You could never walk that distance,' scoffed her husband, but Mrs Barnes declared she would have a darn good try.

Fish, however, suddenly gave in. He said if Floss had got to be put down, then he would rather take her to the vet himself than let anyone else do it, and he would go in tomorrow as his father had arranged. If Mrs Barnes suspected he was up to something, she did not show it, and Mr Barnes was so convinced that Fish was dumb that I suppose it never entered his head.

Fish set off with Floss the next day at eleven o'clock in the morning, with two fifty-pence pieces in his pocket—one from his father to pay the vet, and one from his mother, squeezed from the housekeeping funds, to buy himself a good meal and anything else that he fancied. Fish was seen, alone, at five to five, waiting outside the warehouse where his father worked. Then he, and Floss, disappeared.

Chapter 7

WHEN it first became generally known that Fish was lost, those of us who knew him best were not particularly surprised. Grown-ups were saying, 'James Barnes? That little boy from the Ferns with the dog? Poor little mite, he must have met with an accident.' And when door-to-door gossip revealed the nature of the errand upon which Mr Barnes had sent his son walking into town, there was a great deal of indignation.

But Tom, and Pete, and Gary and I were pretty sure that whatever had happened to Fish, it was not an accident and one or two grown-ups who knew him best, like his stepmother, and Miss Davies, our teacher, had their doubts. When it was discovered that Fish had never turned up at the vet's with Floss at all, other people began to agree with us, and think that Fish must be hiding up somewhere with his precious dog.

But as day followed day, and there was no sign of Fish, we all became mystified, not just the grown-ups, but us boys as well. It was early December—not particularly cold or stormy for the time of year, but quite wintry enough for us to wonder how Fish could be sleeping out and living rough with his dog for days on end without coming to any harm, and he could hardly have been given shelter by anyone in the neighbourhood without their realizing he was wanted.

When Mr Barnes came out of the warehouse, and saw no sign of Fish, he waited around for a while, getting pretty cross, I expect. Then one of his work-mates said he had seen Fish standing by himself at that very spot not five minutes before Mr Barnes appeared. So Mr Barnes hunted around a bit on his motor-bike, and then went home. He probably felt uncomfortable about telling people what Fish was doing in town that day, so he did not ask anyone if they had seen the boy, or leave a message at the warehouse. He said later he assumed somebody else had given the boy a lift home, and his best course was to get back himself and find out what had happened to him.

When he got home, there was no sign of Fish. The last Mrs Barnes had seen of him was when he set off with Floss on his long walk. She told her husband he had better go to the Rhos and Tygwyn to ask if Fish had been seen there.

Mr Barnes was not at all anxious to do that, so first he rode back into town to see if he could have missed Fish somehow, and he was either waiting for him still back at the warehouse or walking home. But there was no sign of him, and when he got back to the Ferns he had still not shown up. So then he had to put his pride in his pocket and come knocking at our doors, asking us if we had seen his son.

He got no information, and scant sympathy, from either my father or Mr Thomas.

Mr Thomas told him he must report it to the police, and offered him the use of the telephone. He could have gone to see Sam in the village, of course, but as Fish had last been seen in town it seemed better to ring the police station there. Mr Barnes was in a fluster over using the phone, so in the end Mr Thomas did it for him. The police sergeant told him he would pass on the information to all the men on duty, asking them to keep a look-out, and if the boy did not turn up at home within two hours Mr Barnes was to ring back and say so, and they would mount a full-scale search.

By dawn next day the search was in full swing. By Tuesday evening, the story of Fish's disappearance was reported on the regional news broadcasts, and by Wednesday there were small paragraphs in some of the daily papers. By the evening, it was headline news. The police, it said, had not ruled out the possibility of foul play. I asked Mum what that meant, and for

94

once she hesitated. Then she said, 'It means they think it is just possible Fish has been murdered.'

That shook me, all right. It surely could not be true? There were one or two things that were beginning to worry me, and I asked Mum if I could go down and see Tom and Gary. I think she knew something of what I was thinking, because she said yes, of course, and if we could think of anything more we could tell the police, then we must go down and see Sam Morgan at once. Then she said something very odd.

'I'll walk down with you as far as the cross-roads,' she said. 'And I think Dad wants to see Mr Thomas about something later, so if you stop on at Tygwyn he can pick you up in the van.' I was rather surprised, but it suited me, so I just said all right. But when Mum turned back at the cross-roads, she said to me again, 'If Dad's a bit late, don't start walking up on your own.'

'Why ever not?' I asked.

She muttered something about Dad going somewhere else in the village, and he might miss me, which seemed daft. There's only one way from Tygwyn to our place unless you cut across the football field, and I was not likely to do that in the dark. Then she said, 'I don't like you running about so much on your own these dark nights,' and went home.

I puzzled a good bit about that remark, because she had never made a fuss about it before. But I was soon at Tygwyn, where I was glad to find Pete because what I wanted to say concerned him as well.

'Here *is* Jimmy,' said Gary as I came in, as though they had been talking about me.

Of course, the police had questioned all us boys very closely about Fish, what he was like, where he used to go, what sort of things he did, whether he had ever said anything to any of us that might give them a clue. Sam Morgan had been up at our place twice, and some detective I did not know had been up as well, and Sam had also visited us in school. I had told Sam about my visit to check on Floss in the night, and about my quarrel with Fish the next morning, though I hadn't liked doing it much. One of the things that made me most miserable about Fish was remembering how we had parted the last time I saw him.

I had *not* told them anything about the reflectors affair. It would not have cleared Floss, because she had every opportunity to chase sheep after we lost her on the way home, and it would have brought trouble on Tom and Pete without throwing much light on where Fish could be now. In any case, for the first couple of days we were not at all sure that we ought to help the police too much. If Fish was trying to hide, and for the best of reasons, it would be pretty unfriendly to set the police on his trail. This feeling began to fade as the days went by, and I realized that even if Fish *had* disappeared on purpose he might now be in real trouble, and on his last visit Sam had explained this side of things very carefully to me. I did not know how Gary felt, but I now thought we ought to tell Sam everything we could.

Tom and Pete and Gary were alone in the living-room when I turned up, but as soon as Tom saw me, he said, 'Come on, let's go up to our bedroom. We can get a bit of peace there.' Although it was only really Tom and Gary I saw much of, there were actually three more Thomas children—Kevin, who was twenty and worked on the farm with his father, and two girls, one at college and one in the sixth form at the secondary school.

As a result, Tygwyn was always full of people. Mostly, if we wanted to be on our own we went out to the barn to talk, but it was cold and dark for that now. We went upstairs and sat around on Gary's and Tom's beds.

'It's about the night you and Fish went up to do the reflectors,' said Tom, without beating about the bush. 'We think you ought to tell Sam about it.' I was glad they saw it the same way as I did, but one thing worried me.

'What if he asks me who put them wrong in the first place?' I said. Actually the real problem was if he didn't ask me, but just assumed that it must have been me and Fish as well. I could not very well go out of my way to put the blame on Tom and Pete, but I certainly did not want people to think I had done it.

'Fair play,' said Tom. 'We'll all go together and we'll tell him the lot.' I admired Tom for that, because he must have been as unhappy about his father thinking he had done it as I was about my father thinking I had. Pete agreed. Oddly enough, the only person who thought we should go on keeping quiet about the whole affair was Gary, who was the only one who had nothing to lose, but nobody took much notice of what he thought.

We went downstairs then, and Tom told his father that we had thought of something we ought to tell Sam about Fish.

Mr Thomas said at once he would ring Sam and no doubt he would come up, which is what happened. Tom looked pretty white about the thought of having to say it all in front of his father as well as Sam, but he said to us, 'It's bound to come out in the end. May as well get it all over at once.'

We told the whole story, and Mr Thomas looked grave and upset, but Sam kept his face blank. He just asked a few questions of fact, as though he were an unknown policeman making enquiries, and that helped. After we had finished, nobody had much to say. Sam couldn't very well lay into Tom and Pete then and there, with Mr Thomas looking on, and nor could Mr Thomas with Sam there, particularly as Pete was Sam's nephew. Funnily enough, the only thing they both blamed them for straight out was not for tampering with the reflectors in the first place, though I expect they had a go at them about that another time, but because they had got Fish and me 'to go and do their dirty work for them', as Mr Thomas put it.

Sam got the point about Floss, but agreed it did not make a great deal of difference. I could have kept quiet about Floss getting separated from us on the way home, but if you decide to make a clean breast of things it is no use holding out on one little part. Anyhow, Sam had some fresh news on the subject of sheep-killing, which was something we had all forgotten about in the excitement of the last few days.

'There's been some sheep killed up at Newbridge, three miles this side of town,' he said. 'Last night, that was.'

'Then that means it wasn't Floss all the time,' I said at once.

'Could do,' said Sam. 'Could just mean it was a different dog this time.'

'Newbridge is some way away,' said Mr Thomas. But Sam had not finished.

'Or it could mean,' he went on, 'that Floss is still around somewhere in that area.'

'Then Fish. . . . ?' I began.

98

'. . . . might be safe and sound somewhere up there, too?' concluded Sam. 'We're working on that.'

'More likely Fish has been murdered and Floss has gone off hunting for food,' suggested Gary, brightly. We all turned to look at him, rather shocked at his tone of voice.

'That will do, Gary,' said Mr Thomas, sharply. He turned to Tom and Pete.

'Mr Morgan and I will be having a talk about your pranks,' he said. 'And no doubt he will be having some more to say to you both about that. And so shall I,' he added fiercely to Tom. Then he looked at me. 'And what,' he asked, 'are we going to say to your mother and father about all this?' I did not know, so I looked at my toes and said nothing.

Mr Thomas patted me on the shoulder. 'I shouldn't worry too much if I were you,' he said. 'I think it would be best if I had a word with your father about it first, seeing as how it was my Tom here that got you into this mess. I don't think young Jimmy is in trouble with the law over this affair, is he, Constable?' I knew then he was joking, because he and Sam Morgan and my father had all been at school together, and he would never have called Sam 'Constable' if he had been serious.

'Not unless I bring a charge of making fools of the police,' said Sam, winking. 'I shan't forget me standing up on that hill shining my torch around when you two rascals were hiding under the bracken and spiriting that dog away from under my very nose.'

I suppose that made us all think of Fish again, because nobody had anything to say for a minute; then Sam went through to the kitchen with Mr Thomas, and soon after we heard a van turn into the yard, and guessed it was my father come to fetch me. We stayed in the living-room and tried to think of something to talk about.

'I suppose it was worth it,' said Pete. 'Uncle Sam didn't seem to think it had much to do with finding Fish now.'

'Oh, well,' said Tom, 'it hadn't, really, but at least your

uncle knows now that Fish wasn't quite the drip that people thought he was.'

'Huh!' said Gary. 'You may have thought so.' Tom asked him what he meant by that, but Gary refused to be drawn.

After a bit, I remembered Mum's funny behaviour when I said I wanted to come down tonight, which was why Dad had come down to get me.

'Lucky he did, then,' said Tom. 'Give 'em a chance to wag their heads over the misdeeds of the younger generation.' He was much more cheerful now the worst was over.

'Yes,' I said, 'but why should Mum want him to come and get me? And walking down with me herself? Did she think I was going to run off after Fish?'

'Not you,' said Gary.

'More likely she was afraid you might get murdered, too,' said Pete.

I stared at him in silence. 'You mean. . . . ?' If that were true, then it could mean all sorts of things. I don't know if I went pale, but I felt it. Tom looked shaken, too, but not Gary.

'That's scared you,' he observed, mockingly.

'Oh, stop being such a stupid nit,' snapped Tom. Gary was certainly being irritating that night, which was unlike him. 'Do you really think, Pete, that Fish has been murdered, and that the murderer is still lurking somewhere around?'

'He doesn't need to be lurking anywhere; he can just be living his normal life,' said Pete.

'Then he wouldn't be *here*,' said Tom.

'Murderers have got to live somewhere. Why not here?'

There was another tense silence, then Tom said, 'Oh, don't be daft, Pete. Who do you suppose would murder Fish around here?'

Because Pete's uncle was a policeman, we were all inclined to treat Pete as an expert on crime, which he rather liked. He seemed to be considering now, and I was not sure how far he was serious.

100

'Well,' he said, 'the most likely person I can think of would be Mr Barnes.'

'But that's his own father!' I cried.

'All the more reason,' said Pete. 'Uncle Sam says that more than half the murders committed in this country are done by close relations of the victim.'

'Yeah,' said Tom. 'I can well believe it. I've often wanted to strangle Gary.' That made us all laugh, and I felt better. I decided Pete had just been teasing—but all the same, the conversation had set a lot of confused thoughts stirring in my mind. I was very glad Dad had come to fetch me home in the van, and I wondered what it was going to feel like having to pass the Ferns on our lonely lane every time I went anywhere.

Then, next morning, before going to school, we heard on the news that a man had been taken into custody in connection with the disappearance of James Barnes, and was helping the police with their enquiries. I asked Dad what that meant. He looked very sober as he explained that it meant the police had traced somebody whom they *thought* might have murdered Fish, and they were trying to get the truth out of him. Beyond making sure that Dan and Jean and I all set off together to go to school, nobody suggested going with us to the cross-roads this time.

Then, when I got to school, I discovered that the man who was helping the police with their enquiries was Mr Barnes.

I went straight home from school that day. I did not feel I wanted to talk to anyone, least of all Gary, who seemed to be enjoying the drama altogether too much for my liking. Unexpectedly, Miss Davies told the car-driver he was to squeeze me in, although it meant taking more children than he was allowed to do, so that I could walk up the lane with Jean and Dan.

As we passed I cast sideways glances at the Ferns, looking silent and blank, and longed to be cosily and safely inside our own home, with just my own family around me. But when I

101

walked into our kitchen the first thing I saw was Dawn and Tracy crawling about on the floor, and Mum making up a bed on the settee in the living-room with Mrs Barnes.

'What are *they* doing here?' asked Dan, looking with some distaste at the little girls. That was exactly what I felt like, so I was glad he had said it for me.

'Mrs Barnes is going to stay with us for a day or two,' said Mum brightly, 'so you'll have someone to play with, Dan. Won't that be nice?'

'They're too little,' said Dan; but after tea he played with Dawn very happily, and Jean made a fuss of Tracy. It was just as well, because Mrs Barnes seemed to be going round in a dream. 'I don't know why you're doing this,' she kept on saying to my mother, over and over again. 'It's very kind of you.'

Mum is rather shy of strangers usually. But today directly Dad came home from the village at dinner-time and told her that it was Mr Barnes who had been taken to the police station, Mum went straight down to the Ferns and swept up a dazed-looking Mrs Barnes and two very grubby children and brought them home.

'It's no trouble at all,' she kept saying to Mrs Barnes. 'There's plenty of room. You can go in the double-bed with the two little ones, and I shall sleep in Jimmy's bed, and he can go in the living-room with his father. There's a settee in there, and a spare mattress I can put on the floor and they'll be as right as rain in there. And I'll only just be along the passage if the kiddies want anything in the night.'

I suppose Dad caught my doleful expression, because he pulled a very comical face at me. I felt better after that.

Mrs Barnes trailed after my mother all evening like a lost dog. It was Jean who bathed Dawn and Tracy and put them to bed—I was surprised how good at it she was, but then Jean likes to be bossing people around. Dan seemed to be feeling a bit left out at this stage, and there did not appear much for me to do, or anywhere for me to sit, so I built Dan a police station with blocks on his bedroom floor—perhaps it was not the most tactful thing to be making, but Dan always wants me to build police stations.

It felt strange, going to bed in the living-room, and though I had never worried before about sleeping on my own, I hoped it would not be long before Dad came to bed—but I was surprised when he did come, because it really was *very* soon.

'You're early,' I said.

'A farmer's always ready for bed,' said Dad. Then he added, 'Mrs Barnes has had a lot of worries lately. I reckon now the kids are asleep she'd like a chance to have a chat with your mother, and she'll do better without me hanging around like a spare part.' In less than five minutes he was snoring.

I felt much too disturbed to go to sleep. The settee was too narrow and had odd lumps; it felt peculiar sleeping on the ground floor, and a great wide wedge of light shone through over the badly-fitting door that led into the kitchen. Then there was Dad's snoring. But above all, something was hurting in my chest, like a voice crying out for a lost friend. Only today had I really begun to believe that Fish might indeed be dead, murdered even, and murdered by . . .

I became aware of voices next door.

I heard my mother say, 'I expect your husband will be home tomorrow, but you're welcome to let the children stay here as long as you like.'

'D'you think they will? Let him out?'

My mother could not help being truthful. 'Well, I suppose that depends. . . .' she began.

'Depends on whether he done it, you mean?' Mrs Barnes suddenly broke into noisy crying, that went on and on. That shocked me. I had always thought that grown-ups just did not cry like that, not ever, not even when their son was feared dead and their husband accused of murder; I thought you left off wanting to cry when you grew up.

But Mrs Barnes cried and cried, and through her crying

she was telling Mum how of course Willie never done it, he
could never do such a thing, but nobody would ever believe
him because he had such a funny way with him, he didn't
know how to talk to people straight, like they was his friends,
but if you really lived with him, then you *knew* he'd never do
a thing like that; and she knew people found it hard to like her
Willie, and he wasn't very bright at understanding people, but
he was really very fond of Jimmy (oh, yeah? I thought) and
Mrs Barnes went on, about how when she was first living with
Mr Barnes and expecting her first baby—Dawn—this little
boy of seven was landed on her, whom she didn't know at
all, and she didn't know anything about little boys anyway
and she couldn't be bothered with him much, because she was
so wrapped up in Dawn, and then Tracy, and she kind of got
used to having him around without paying him much attention, beyond feeding him and washing his clothes, and it was
only lately she had begun to understand him and want to help
him and do things for him and . . .

There was a lot more, and a lot of the same stuff over and
over again. At first, as I say, I was shocked and a bit frightened, but later, when she had quietened down and just went
on and on in the same low tired voice, with my mother making
soothing noises every now and again, it began to make me
sleepy. And before I knew what had happened I had dropped
off completely, and slept like a log until the morning.

Chapter 8

NEXT morning we were all having breakfast, except Mrs Barnes who was still sleeping, and Jean was feeding Tracy and Mum telling her not to bother because it was time we got off to school, when there was a knock at the door. I went to open it, and there stood Mr Barnes.

'Hullo, Jimmy,' he said. 'Is my wife here?' I just stood gaping, but Mum called over my shoulder,

'Is that you, Mr Barnes? Come on in.'

I stood well aside to let him pass me, and Mr Barnes pulled off his cap and stood wiping his feet on the mat, and stammering, 'I f-found your note, found your note, Mrs Price. This is very kind of you, very kind indeed.'

'Come along and have a cup of tea,' said my mother. 'I don't know whether you've had any breakfast, but I dare say you could do with some. Get *along*, Jean, go and get your coat on for school. There, Mr Barnes, if you sit right there by Tracy maybe you could give her the rest of her cereal. Your wife will be down in a minute, but I told her to have a good lie-in this morning. Get a move on, Jimmy, do; you'll never be in time for school if you just stand there. Help Dan into his anorak.'

It was all very strange. So far as I know Mum had never exchanged two words with Mr Barnes, and now she was fussing over him as if—as if he was one of the family, I was going to say, except she never fusses over us like that.

'Goodbye, then,' I said coldly. 'Come on, Dan.'

'Wait for me,' called Jean, struggling into her coat. As I stood waiting to shut the door behind Jean I heard Mum say, 'Is everything all right, then?'

I hung on then, with the door not quite closed, although Jean had run through and was catching up Dan across the yard, so was able to hear Mr Barnes say, 'Well, they haven't found any trace of James, no trace at all. But they've let me go, if that's what you mean.' He laughed, nervously. 'All the questions they kept asking, and the way they went on keeping me there to answer them, anyone would think they suspected *me* of having a hand in it. I said to them, I said, "You go on keeping me here like this and people will be thinking I murdered my own son next." They didn't even apologize—very unfeeling, I thought they were, that lot up at the station, but I suppose it's a job to them, just like any other. But I will say, they let me go soon after that. Thanked me for helping them, they did; well, they could hardly do no less.'

I closed the door very gently and ran off after the others.

I felt thoroughly muddled and confused. Were we all wrong to have suspected Mr Barnes of being a murderer? Should we leave off suspecting him now? I did not know who to believe, or who to blame. Ordinary people often did little things that were wrong, like Tom and the reflectors. Then there was Fish, always telling lies. Did one draw the line between Tom and Fish, and if so, who were on which side of it? What about Mrs Barnes, admitting she did not look after Fish properly? And what about Mr Barnes? What indeed?

As I was the only person, apart from Jean and Dan, who knew that Mr Barnes had come home again, I was the centre of attention when I got to school. The only person who did not seem particularly interested was Gary. He had been rather off-hand about the whole affair all along, and it crossed my mind that he was jealous, because the police and everyone had been paying much more attention to me than to him, as though they all knew that I was the one most likely to be in Fish's confidence.

When all the excitement subsided and Miss Davies called us to assembly, Gary whispered to me, 'I've got something important to talk to you about. Will you ask Miss Davies for permission to go to the shop?' I thought he was being rather melodramatic, but I agreed because I was curious.

We older ones were allowed to go to the village shop in the dinner-break if we came from some way out and we said our mothers wanted us to get something for them, but we had to ask permission at roll-call, immediately after assembly.

I put up my hand. 'Please, Miss Davies, can I go to the shop?'

'Yes, Jimmy, that'll be all right. Is there anyone else?'

'Me, please, Miss Davies,' said Gary. Miss Davies did look a bit suspicious then, but nobody else wanted to go, so she let it pass.

The school is a little way out of the main village, across the bridge. Instead of coming straight into the village, you can turn down the short cut to the Llandewi-fach road, which runs alongside the stream at this point. You only have to slip down the bank then, and there's a patch of shingle, unless the water is very high, sheltered by arching tree roots and tucked away beneath the river-bank. If you want to have a private conversation in school time, that's the place to go.

'Well,' I said, as we settled down, 'what is it?'

Gary spun a stone across the water. 'Last time I came here,' he said, 'was with Fish. On Monday,' he added after a pause.

It was on Monday that Fish had missed school to take Floss to town.

'He wasn't in school on Monday.'

'No,' said Gary. 'But he was here.'

'Here? Have you told the police?'

'No, and I don't intend to. And if I'm to tell you any more, you've got to promise not to tell the police, either.'

'Have you got any more to tell?'

'Plenty; but I'm not going to say a word of it until you promise not to tell anyone—not the police, not your parents, not Tom even, not *anyone*.'

'Look,' I said. 'If it's to do with Fish, it's serious, not a game. We've tried not telling grown-ups things lately, and it has landed us in a right mess, more often than not. I won't tell anyone if I can possibly help it. But I can't promise, without knowing what it is all about. It might be a matter of life and death.'

I thought Gary would mock me, being so righteous about it, but he looked quite serious. 'All right,' he said. 'You promise not to tell anyone anything I am going to tell you, unless it looks like becoming a matter of life and death.'

I promised.

'I know where Fish is,' said Gary.

'*You* know where he is?' I repeated, dazedly. 'You mean, you know he's not dead?'

'I know where he is, and I know he's not dead; not Floss, either,' said Gary. 'At least, he was fine two days ago.'

Two days ago. That was Wednesday.

'Look, Gary,' I said carefully, because actually I was feeling angry for all sorts of reasons and some of them were better than others, 'for days now not only have the police been hunting all the time, but all the neighbours, and your father, and my father, and everyone has been worried sick, and what about Mrs Barnes crying all last night at our place, and Mr Barnes with everyone thinking he's a murderer? Why didn't you say you knew where he was?'

'Because I promised,' said Gary simply. 'Same as you've promised me.' That silenced me. Gary went on then. 'Fish needs help,' he said. 'Up to now, I've been helping him, but it's not safe for me to help him any more.'

'You?' I said. 'You!' I wanted to say 'Why not me?' but I didn't.

'If I tell you the rest, will you stick by your promise?'

I took a deep breath. 'Yes,' I said.

'Good,' said Gary. 'You know,' he added, 'it wasn't just that Fish was angry because he had quarrelled with you, or because he didn't trust you, but he said if he disappeared the first person they would come and ask would be you, and it would be much more difficult for you to pretend you knew nothing than it would for me. Which is quite right.'

That made me feel a bit better.

'Go on,' I said. 'Tell me the rest. It will be the end of play-time soon.'

'When I left the farm to go to school on Monday morning, Fish was waiting for me. I was already late, so Fish told me to meet him here, like we done today. When I got here, Fish was here already, with Floss, and he told me all about his father saying Floss must be destroyed, and the sheep-killing, and all that. He said his mum thought he was already on his way to town but of course he wasn't going to take Floss to the vet's, and he would just have to go into hiding with her until something turned up. He asked me to help him, and naturally I said I would. I thought it would be fun.'

In that sort of way Gary is like Fish. He is always ready for a lark, and doesn't worry what other people will think, or whether it is going to worry his parents, or be dangerous.

Gary went on. 'We arranged that we would hide Floss in our bottom barn, and Fish would walk into town by himself, just hoping nobody who knew him would see him without

Floss. He had already walked the first mile *with* Floss, and doubled back through the fields, to put people off the scent—for instance, my brother Kevin was hedging on the roadside that morning, and he saw Fish go by with Floss, and told the police so. Afterwards, Fish went back through the fields that first mile, and then on by road. When he got to town he bought dog biscuits and dried dog meat, and some ordinary biscuits and stuff for himself, and then he went to the warehouse. His first plan was to come home with his father, and later slip out and join Floss. But he was a bit worried in case his father wanted to know why his duffle-bag was so full of stuff, and just then he noticed a furniture van pulled up for petrol at the garage across the road which had the name of the firm on one side and a Cardiff address. He had thought of hitching a lift before, but was put off in case he was picked up by someone local, who would give the show away, but this Cardiff van seemed safe enough, so he walked across and asked for a lift—I expect he told a few fibs, you know Fish—and got the driver to put him down just beyond the school.

'From there he walked along the stream to the back bridge, and so over to Bottom Barn, without much danger of meeting anyone. There's plenty of hay in the barn, and I slipped him a couple of old blankets down there. He had Floss, and he had food, and had only to pop down to the brook for water, and it was quite warm. He was pretty happy and comfortable there, one way and another.'

'But surely,' I interrupted, 'someone would look there when all that search was going on?'

'That's what we were most afraid of, so that's when we did the daringest thing of all. We knew they'd be searching, first thing in the morning, so I said I'd actually suggest the barn, so that they would go there right away, and Fish could hide somewhere else, and then come back again when they'd been there. The question was, where?'

'Where?' I asked, as that seemed to be what Gary was hoping I would say.

'In our stock-lorry!' said Gary. 'On the top layer.' Mr Thomas was one of the few farmers round us who had a stock-lorry—most of us made do with the back of the van and it smelt like it!—but if anyone needed to move a really big lot of stock, then they borrowed Mr Thomas's lorry. You could put up two layers, apart from the floor, for carrying sheep. For cattle or horses, of course, the middle layer was removed, but not usually the top one. It was there, Gary told me, that Fish and Floss hid, slipping up in the early dawn before a search of the area was started.

'It worked out even better than we had hoped,' said Gary, 'because Kevin had brought half-a-dozen ponies into the stable the night before, ready to load and take down to Carmarthenshire first thing in the morning—and that's just what he did. He was off before anybody knew the hunt for Fish was seriously on, and didn't get back till late afternoon—the lorry passed me as I was coming home from school. I went into the house and soon found out the police had searched all our land once, and made a thorough check of Bottom Barn—Fish had brought the blankets up to the stock-lorry, so that was all right. All I had to do was nip out while everyone was still at tea and tell Fish, and he went back to the barn.'

'And he'd been all the way to Carmarthenshire and back?'

'Yeah. He was feeling pretty sick and miserable too, by then. So I went down with him, and we talked, and I went back and nicked some sausages and matches and stuff, and we lit a fire and cooked them.'

'Somebody might have seen the smoke!' I exclaimed.

'They didn't though. It was a bit of fun. I wished I could sleep out with him—I think he wished it too, although he'd got Floss, but we knew it would be stupid. I think he was O.K. that night, but next day things began to get difficult. The police began searching all over everywhere again, poking about, you know, and you never knew where they'd be next. That was Wednesday. I was in a panic all day at school in case they found him, and when I was going back home past the police house, I heard an inspector asking a policeman if he had checked Bottom Barn again, and he said yes, but not thoroughly because of all the bales of hay in it, and the inspector said go and do it thoroughly, and told another chap to go and help him move all the bales.

'I nipped off pretty sharp then, and got to the barn, and told Fish what I'd heard. He was feeling fairly happy because he'd watched them sweep the hillside opposite and down to the stream, and then carry on from this side and up to the farm, and hid in the middle of the bales when he saw them coming, so now he thought he was safe.

'Meantime, in school, I'd been thinking of a better hiding-place, and hit on something. You know that cottage right up in the hills beyond Llandewi, that's ours, and Mum lets out to tourists in the summer? Nobody goes near the place in the winter. Fish could live there for days, light a fire and everything, and nobody would ever know. So I told him about it, and how to get there, as best as I could, and he hopped it, and I hopped it, because we could see them two policemen coming across the next field.'

'But what will he live *on*, even if he finds the place?' I asked.

'That's just it,' said Gary. 'I said I'd ride over on my bike tonight, and take him food or money; but the trouble is, I can't.'

'I can,' I said, without a thought; then I wished I hadn't. 'Why can't you?' I added, hastily.

'Because that time Fish had to leave a blanket behind—he couldn't carry two, and I couldn't take one home because I would be in full view of the police. We should have hidden it down by the stream, but we were in an awful hurry and didn't have time to think. Also I'd been taking bones and stuff down for Floss, and the silly dog had hidden them under the hay. Ten minutes later the police walked in, and found the blanket, and the fire remains, and the bones and other bits and pieces. Fish had slipped out behind the barn and crossed the stream and was hiding in the bracken on the far side by then. I managed not to be seen by the barn, but I'd been seen going in that direction, and coming home late, and later on that evening that inspector came up and asked an awful lot of questions. I said we'd picknicked in that barn sometimes, with Fish, but not in the last week. All the same, they're watching me all the time.'

'Now?' I asked, anxiously.

'I hope not,' said Gary. 'That's why I wanted to talk to you in school time, not afterwards. But we must get back now.' He looked cautiously down the lane again. 'Come on,' he said, 'I can explain the rest as we go.'

'The rest' was quite simple, and just as I had feared. Gary handed me just over two pounds, which he had been saving for a new bike. I was to slip out as soon as it was safe—that was becoming a habit!—take Tom's bike (Gary's was a bit small for me) and ride for all I was worth up past Llandewi-fach and on another six miles up the lonely little valley that led to Cwmdu, which was what the cottage was called. There I would find Fish, see if he was all right and give him the money—food would have been better, but neither of us could see how I could buy food on a deserted road in the middle of the night, but I could buy a few things from our shop on the way home from school without exciting suspicion.

'What would be best,' said Gary, 'would be if you could leave him Tom's bike.'

'I'd never get home in time,' I said.

'No,' said Gary. 'Unless—unless Fish came half-way back with you, and then rode back while you walked the rest.'

'I'll have to see how the time goes,' I said. 'It's not going to help Fish or anyone if I'm caught out hiking down the Llandewi road at five o'clock in the morning.'

It's funny, because this was a far bigger thing than the reflectors affair, and yet I felt much less nervous about it. We were already back at the school, but everybody was still tearing round the playground. It's amazing how much can happen in half an hour, sometimes, and how little, others. I looked at my watch to see if there was still time to go to the shop, but there wasn't.

Two things did worry me, though. 'What will Fish think when he sees me and knows you've told me all this? Won't he be cross?'

' "Don't tell anyone," he told me, but then he said, "and if you do have to, then tell Jimmy, but make him promise not to tell anyone else first." He said you were too trusting, and you are, Jim. And tell him,' Gary added, 'about the sheep-killing at Newbridge. It was the night Fish was walking from here to Cwmdu, and so I don't reckon it could have been Floss. If any

114

more sheep are killed in that direction, then they'll have to stop blaming her, I should think.'

'And then he can come home,' I said. It all seemed so simple.

'One other thing,' I added. 'Supposing something happens—might be even a puncture or something—and I don't get home before they discover I'm missing. Will you tell my parents I'm all right?'

'Yeah,' said Gary. 'I'll do that. I don't mind old Barnes shivering in his shoes for a week or so thinking his son has been murdered—might buck him up a bit, don't you think?—but I wouldn't let that happen to your dad and mum, honest I wouldn't, even if it meant giving Fish away, though it probably wouldn't come to that.'

The school bell rang just then, and we went back to our class-room. I was too busy making plans to pay much attention, but I was feeling pretty happy.

Chapter 9

I CALLED in at the shop on the way home, having persuaded Miss Davies that there was no need for me to ride up in the school car. I could not possibly spend over two pounds on food without Mrs Burns thinking I was up to something very odd, but I was able to lay in some bars of chocolate and some candles (that was Gary's idea—Mrs Burns thought Mum must have been expecting an electricity cut) and some soup packets (Gary's idea again) and some cheese and sardines and biscuits and apples.

Just before I got home I realized candles were not much use without matches. I wondered if Fish had some still, but decided to nick a box just in case. I took some bread while I was at it.

Luckily Mrs Barnes had gone back to the Ferns, taking Tracy. Dawn had stayed on with us, because she was happy and Mum said it would be more of a rest for her mother, but Mum and Dad had gone back to their room, and I was back in mine, which made my get-away easy. Gary had said he would play around the yard on Tom's bicycle if he could and leave it accidentally-on-purpose leaning against the gate at the bottom of the short drive where it comes out on to the lane to save me coming into the yard.

Everything went fine, except that as I emerged from the dairy door carrying a rather heavier load than I would have wished, I was greeted by the steady downward drift of snowflakes! Here was a do, I felt, but then I saw it was not really lying, and remembered we were unlikely to get a heavy fall of snow in early December. I trotted down the lane very cautiously past the Ferns, because there was still a light on in

116

an upstairs window, and so down to the Tygwyn turn, where I found Tom's bike, nicely pumped up and ready. I peered around anxiously for a glimpse of one of those detectives Gary fancied watched his every move, but saw none. Then I was on that bike and away.

One thing worried me now. If it had been difficult for Fish and me to take cover when surprised by an oncoming car, how much more difficult on a bicycle! However, luck was with me, luck and the snowstorm. For the snow had not died away; far from it, the flakes came steadily falling, whitening my knees and shoulders, fluttering into my face like a cloud of moths, wriggling into the crannies between my anorak hood and my face, and between my sleeves and my wrists. I could feel it clinging wetly to my hair and eyebrows, and, as I got higher up and it began to lie on the road, I felt the added pull on the bicycle. It was also getting steep, and I soon had to get off and walk.

I slogged on, past the famous bend, beginning to feel thoroughly anxious about the turn the weather had taken. But then the ground eased out, and I was able to mount the bike again, and though I could hear the soft snow crunching beneath my wheels in the black silence, I felt unconcerned, because I was spinning along pretty fast. It did not take me long to reach Llandewi-fach, a hamlet sleeping under a quilt of snow.

If I had been on foot I would have crept around the village by the fields, but you can't do that with a bicycle in the middle of the night in a snow-storm. I stopped on the outskirts, and no one was in sight, so I rode boldly through. When I glanced back on the other side, to see if anyone had seen me, all was quiet, but straight down the clean whiteness of the road led a single narrow track—left by my bicycle. Instead of praying for the snow to stop, I began to wish it would come down even faster to hide my tracks—and that is exactly what it did.

I did not realize this at first, because I was going along at a great rate, or so it seemed to me—distance and slopes can be very misleading when your only guide is a little bobbing cycle-lamp focused waveringly through the snow-flakes on a small circle of white road three yards in front of you. Then I noticed that a wind had got up, and was blowing me along on a wall of snowflakes—that is, until the first of the right-hand turns that was to take me to Cwmdu.

I had been to Cwmdu with the Thomas family in the spring, when they had spent occasional days up there putting it in order for the summer tourists—Gary and I had great fun, climbing on the hills and trying to tickle trout in the mountain stream, while Mrs Thomas and the two daughters swept and aired and made beds, but I began to realize that a journey by car on a bright spring day is very different from one by night in a snow-storm on a bicycle.

This first right-hand turn I was sure about—it was the later ones I felt more doubtful over. The trouble was that the lane now climbed steeply and steadily, without hedges, veering round until it took me into the face of the blizzard. Almost at once I had to dismount and trudge along, forcing the wheels through an ever-deepening layer of soft snow. I remembered the road climbed right up over a high rounded ridge and then swung left, dropping by degrees into the bottom of a little upland valley that rose to meet the road as it edged itself down the side of the hill. I thought I must stick to the bike, although now it was a terrible drag, because I still had at least five miles to go, and once I got over the ridge I hoped the downward slope would make it possible for me to ride along easily through the snow.

Nagging at the back of my mind was the question, 'How am I going to get home through this?' But as soon as I asked myself whether I ought not to turn back straightaway and give up hope of getting through to Fish, I knew there was no question of that. For one thing, I simply could not face the seven miles—eight miles by now—home again without a rest in some sheltered place. For another, I was getting worried about Fish. Gary had talked gaily about Fish living for weeks at the holiday cottage, cooking for himself, sleeping in a comfortable bed and so forth—but then Gary saw the cottage in his mind much as I had imagined it—bright and clean and gay in the spring sunshine, being polished up by his mother and sisters. Now, in the cold snow-filled darkness, I imagined Fish with no candles, no matches, perhaps, no fuel for the fire even if he was able to light it and keep it alight, and no food to cook on it even if he were able to cook. It was a very lonely place, even if he had Floss for company; I was beginning to feel pretty lonely myself, and I had only been out for half one night; Fish had been on his own, sleeping rough and snatching cold mouthfuls of food when he could, for over five days.

The steepness of the hill had eased a little, and though I was now in the teeth of the gale, and wet through from driving snow, I took heart, feeling that I was over the hump of the ridge, and would be starting the downward slope into the comparative shelter of the valley. And then, I met the hardest blow of all. I swung up on to the bike, pushing through several inches' depth of snow hoping to get enough way on to carry me through the clinging stuff—and rode straight into a drift that clogged the front wheel up to the hub. I tumbled off into the snow, which was soft and welcoming as a bed, and staggered out of it more like a snowman than a boy.

I pulled the bike out of the drift, and tried across on the right-hand side of the road. Here it was a little better, but quite impossible to ride through. I half-pushed, half-carried the bicycle a short distance, but soon realized it was hopeless. The snow had been drifting into the lane on this side of the hill all night, and any more cycling was out of the question. I dropped the bike by the side of the road, and plodded on. I remember thinking I should have hidden it, but being too tired to care. I think I had already decided underneath that at the first sign of a farm or cottage, I would go and ask for shelter. By the time I had toiled down to the bottom, I had not only openly decided to do this, but reckoned that Gary's 'matter of life or death' agreement allowed me to get help for Fish, too.

Here I was faced with a fork, and after a little hesitation, took the right-hand one. I walked along faster now, partly driven by panic, partly helped by the high hedges which kept the snow away a bit, and began to hope I was getting near Cwmdu. I seemed to remember there should be a bridge half a mile before the cottage, and a turning to the left immediately after crossing the bridge. If instead of turning left you went straight on, you came almost immediately into the yard of a small farm. I could not make up my mind whether, when I got to the bridge, I should turn left to the cottage, or make for the farm. But, in any case, where was the bridge?

I was just beginning to panic, when I came upon the bridge. At least, it looked like the bridge—but there was no left turn immediately beyond it. It must be round the next corner, I told myself. Finding the bridge had cheered me and I decided that what would seem a very little distance in a car would seem a lot further for a small tired boy walking in a snow-storm in the night. I shifted my bag from one shoulder to the other, for the hundredth time, and took the bicycle lamp—which I had brought with me—in my other hand, and trudged on. I would make for the farm, I decided. Half a mile was just too far to walk.

I must have walked another mile, though, before I ever came to that turn. By the time I had got there, I knew full well I was completely and utterly lost—and completely and utterly exhausted as well. The turning was not the one I remembered—although the road was thickly covered with snow, I knew by the feel of it, and the narrowness of it, that it was little more than a cart-track, and seldom used. Most probably both tracks led to long-abandoned farmhouses—nobody might ever come this way for months on end. I sat down at the side of the road in despair. As if it were someone else far away, I heard my own voice crying for help. Silly fool, my own mind said sleepily, there's no one to hear; but still I could hear my own voice crying like Dan when he has a nightmare, for Mum.

I was just dropping off into a state that was more like a faint than sleep, when I was roused by something warm and wet and hairy, pushing me and licking me, and scratching at me. It was Floss!

'Floss!' I said. 'Floss! Floss!' It was all I could say, over and over again. She started to walk away from me, then. I called her back, panic-stricken, and she came running back and rubbed herself all over me again, with more licking and scratching. She felt so warm and alive—but where had she come from? Where was Fish?

Then it suddenly dawned on me that she must have heard my crying—in which case she must have been quite near, and Fish too. Had they found some shelter? I struggled to my feet, and hung on to Floss to help me. I was for starting off straight away, but Floss nuzzled at my bag, which was already half-covered in snow. I believe she would have carried it if she could. I picked it up, and staggered after her. Little more than a hundred yards brought us to a group of derelict farm buildings. The house itself, in my dim torch-light, looked empty but at least it was standing up, and had a roof on. The door

121

was shut, though not fastened and Floss leapt in through a broken window alongside.

My hand was on the door, to push it open, when I paused, as a fearful thought struck me. Why had Floss alone come out to find me? If Fish was in there, why hadn't he at least opened the door for her, or come to look himself? Would I find Fish in there, and if so, *how would I find Fish*?

I was so frightened to open the door to go in, and so tired, that I almost let myself slide down in a huddle against it in the drifting snow, and just lie there; but as I leant wearily against it the door creaked and swung open suddenly, almost throwing me into the dank little farm kitchen. There was a quick scuffle in the corner, a frightened gasp, and a voice cried hoarsely, 'Who's there?' I swung the torch round. It fell upon a mound of hay piled against the peeling wallpaper, and a duffle bag, familiar even in that lightning glance; I raised the beam, and it shone full upon Fish's face, rising startled out of the tangled hay, tear-streaked and pale beneath the dirt.

'Who is it?' he gasped again, and I realized that I had spoken never a word, and stood in a daze masked behind the the beam from my own torch.

'It's me: Jimmy. Jimmy Price.'

Fish was out of that hay in an instant, clutching at me with tight nervous fingers. 'Oh, Jimmy. I'm glad you've come, Jimmy.'

I said nothing, for I was in a dream of weariness. 'Jimmy, you won't leave me, will you?' I shook my head, for I could not get my tongue round words, and how to explain that I could no more walk another step than I could fly?

'You won't go, will you, Jimmy?' Fish repeated. In the darkness he could not see my gesture.

'No,' I muttered. 'I want to go to bed.' That straw looked the most inviting bed I had ever set eyes on. I tried to stagger towards it.

'We'll get in together and then we'll both be warm. I'm cold, now; are you cold, Jimmy? I've been cold for so long, and so lonely. I'm glad you've come; I'm glad you've come, Jimmy. Is it snowing still? It was snowing when I went to bed. Jimmy, have you got anything to eat? I'm so hungry. Have you got some food, Jimmy? I've only got dog biscuits. What is there, Jimmy? Jimmy, are you all right? What's the matter, Jim? Why don't you answer?' He took the torch out of my hand—I could feel it dropping anyway, but my hand felt so far away from my brain that there did not seem any point telling my hand to go on holding it. Then I was aware of the beam in my face, dazzling me.

'Gosh, Jimmy,' came a distant voice that sounded like Fish's, 'you look fagged out. Come on; I'll help you into bed and you can eat in there.' He steered me over a barricade of bales into a deep well of soft-piled loose hay.

'You're awful wet,' came the distant voice. 'Best take off your anorak and trousers.'

'Can't,' I muttered. Fish tugged about me manfully; I wished he would leave me in peace, but he meant well. I didn't mind the anorak coming off, because I had thick dry woollies—mostly dry anyway, except for the wrists and neck —underneath, but when Fish began to pull off my clammy trousers, I tried to cling on to them.

'I'm cold,' I gasped, through chattering teeth.

'You'll be warmer without them,' said Fish. I thought I had come to rescue Fish, but now, it seemed it was he who was rescuing me. 'We'll wrap up together in the blanket, and put lots of hay on top, and Floss will lie on top of it and we'll soon be as warm as toast. Can I see what food you've brought? You have brought some, haven't you?'

'Yes,' I muttered; 'but don't eat it all now. Some of it's got to be cooked.' I don't know why, but I felt sleepily that it would be terrible if Fish gulped down the dry soup powders. I couldn't eat anything myself—Fish could have the chocolate and the bread and the biscuits for all I cared—but as I plunged into a long, long tunnel of sleep I was thinking how lovely it would be to wake up to a bowl of hot soup.

After that, I was vaguely conscious of Fish burrowing away in my bag, making spurts of conversation and munching happily, and then spells of deep unconsciousness from which I roused once or twice shivering cold, and then the beginning of a spreading glow of warmth. After that I knew no more until Fish woke me in broad daylight. There was a smoky smell in the air, which was surprisingly warm, and I could hear a crackling sound. My first thought was that the place must be on fire, but it wasn't, quite.

'Do wake up, Jimmy,' said Fish. He sounded panicky. 'I'm a bit scared of the fire, and I've burnt my finger.'

There was a great fire roaring up the chimney but as I watched a sudden gust sent not only a thick puff of smoke into the room, but also red flames spilling out over the walls.

'Hey,' I said, 'that looks a bit dangerous.' All the same, it was lovely and warm. 'How did you find wood to burn?'

Fish told me he had found a great heap of wood stored away in one of the outhouses yesterday, but had not been able to light a fire before because his matches were soaked. 'Do you think it's all right?' he asked anxiously.

'Better let it burn down a little,' I said. Apart from the wood, Fish seemed to have been stoking it with hay.

'I wanted to get a fire going before you woke up,' he said. 'We'll have to get your trousers dry somehow.' He had laid two bales at angles in front of the fire, and on one my anorak was spread out, and on the other my trousers. I realized that some of what I had taken to be smoke was the steam rising from my wet clothes.

'You've been busy,' I remarked, climbing right out of my cosy well. It was only a tiny kitchen, and the blazing fire really had warmed it up—even standing there in my pants and socks I did not feel cold. I did feel hungry, though. I looked at my watch. Twenty past two in the afternoon.

'How long have you been up?' I asked. Long enough to have eaten up all the rest of the food? I thought anxiously. But Fish's answer was reassuring. He must have been pretty

125

tired himself, because he said he did not think he had been awake more than an hour. He had not thought to look at my watch, having lived so long with dawn and nightfall as his only time-keepers, but he had only eaten some biscuits, intending to have a feast with me when I woke up.

We got our feast, too, the best meal I have ever tasted. We could not bring ourselves to leave off eating while we were still hungry in order to save our rations, but it did make us very careful to make the best use of what we had got. Fish had not eaten a hot meal since those sausages cooked with Gary on Tuesday evening. Today was Saturday. When I arrived in the night he had got through a bar of chocolate, half a packet of biscuits and an apple and during the morning he had nibbled at the remaining biscuits. I helped him finish those off while we were preparing the feast. We still had two more packets of biscuits, the cheese, three soup packets, a tin of sardines, three apples, and the hunk of bread.

Fish went and fetched some water from the stream in a polythene bag. Apart from a small plastic mug, it was the only container we had, and Fish treated it with the greatest care. He seemed to know his way around the immediate neighbourhood—where to find the wood, and the water—and I realized I had heard nothing of his adventures, or how he, as well as I, had chanced to stumble on this deserted farmhouse.

The fire had burnt lower, and there was a lovely bright glow, with only small flames. Of course we had no saucepan, but I remembered something Tom had told me about boiling water in tinfoil, so I thought why not soup? With my penknife I slit open the top of the soup packet, having read the instructions with great care, and also made two small holes near the top of each side. Fish found a good stick to poke through the holes. Then he poured in water from his polythene bag while I stirred and then we hung it over the fire. It wasn't at all easy to hold it over the fire in such a way that the supporting stick did not burn through, or the packet tear at the holes, or the whole thing tip up. It was almost impossible to watch all those things and still be able to get at it well enough to stir it properly as it came to the boil, which is what it said on the packet, and in any case we had to make it much too thick because we had no room for more water. We got round that by tipping the first brew into the mug and boiling up some more water in the packet, but then we found it difficult to mix the two up because both the containers were full and Fish was afraid it might melt his precious polythene bag to use that. Anyway we sipped a bit and topped it up, and sipped and topped, until it was all gone. It was lumpy, watery in places and burnt in places, lukewarm or scalding—and absolutely delicious.

Encouraged by our cooking success, we proceeded to stick hunks of bread on sticks—cut with a penknife, you could not call them slices—and toasted them, and did the same with knobs of cheese. We even tried toasting ginger biscuits—Fish declared they were much nicer like that, but I was not convinced. We finished off with an apple and half a bar of chocolate each, and washed it all down with stream water.

Then, and only then, we lay back upon our bed of hay, and talked.

Fish, it seemed, had got even more lost than I had on his journey from Llanwern. He had never been to Cwmdu, and only had Gary's hurried instructions to go on. Also he was walking all the way, unlike me with Tom's bicycle. As a result, it took him much longer. He had run off from Bottom Barn at about four o'clock on Wednesday afternoon. It was broad daylight then, and the police were looking for him, although not on the Aberdulais land because they had already searched that in the morning. So he stuck around on the lower slopes, where there was plenty of bracken to give him cover, until it got dark, and then struck off for Llandewi, but still keeping to the slopes below the road because it was only early evening and there would be a fair amount of traffic on the road. By the time he got to Llandewi it was not particularly late—about nine p.m.—but he was getting tired. He skirted round Llandewi by the fields, and found a barn on the far side to rest in. He fell asleep, and when he woke, although it was still dark, he could see the faint streak of dawn. He scuttled off—the barn was much too close to Landewi to make a safe day-time hide-out, especially as he had no idea whether it was in daily use—hoping to get off up the first right-hand turn for Cwmdu before dawn broke, but he missed it because at the time he was cutting through fields on the opposite side of the road. Before he realized it, his quiet road was joined by a much bigger one, heading back to our market town from the north.

He knew then that he had gone wrong, and turned back, but by the time he found the turning it was broad daylight. He saw the lane climbing straight and naked over the bare mountain, with not a hedge, not a tree, to hide behind, and dared not go. Instead, he scrambled away from the road on the opposite side, where at least there were plenty of overgrown hedges and fingers of bracken and undergrowth, until he came to a little wood in the hollow of the valley. Here he lurked about all day, sharing dog biscuits with Floss and opening his last tin of luncheon meat. There was a boggy little brook for water, but nowhere that offered the kind of shelter you get in a hay-filled barn, so he did not sleep.

As soon as darkness fell, he climbed back out of his valley and followed the bare road over the ridge that I was to plod along so wearily twenty-four hours later. It was not snowing then, and he made faster progress than me, but with no better luck. He also took a wrong turn—not, at that time, the same one as I had, but it meant he wandered for miles getting more and more lost, and despairing of ever finding Cwmdu. By the time he stumbled upon this deserted farm he had lost all sense of direction, distance or time, and had come to it not by the lane as I had, but over the open country.

It was still dark when he got there early on Friday morning. He had dropped his torch in a bog, his matches were wet and useless and he must have been no less exhausted and despairing than I was when I arrived the next night. He did have one great advantage over me—Floss. All through his wanderings she was warmth and companionship and comfort to him.

Fish had not spent that first night in the dank little kitchen, which at that time was completely bare. He had gone there because it was the only entrance he could make out in the darkness, but Floss, used by now to living in barns, went exploring and soon led her master to the outbuilding full of bales that seemed to her the proper place to sleep. He was certainly warmer there than he would have been in the house, but still not warm enough to sleep sound. He woke at dawn, feeling thoroughly miserable.

I do not know whether he consciously decided to spend that day in making himself comfortable, or whether he just kept on putting off the moment when he started on his endless wanderings. At any rate, by nightfall he was still there, and had done some sensible things. He had scouted around the immediate neighbourhood, finding no signs of life, but discovering the nearby stream and all the brushwood in another tumbledown outbuilding. Then he had heaved no less than eight bales into the kitchen. By putting two against the damp wall, end to end, and two crossways at head and feet, and two more end to end to complete the rectangle, he had a snug, sheltered cabin. Then he pulled the remaining two bales to pieces, and piled the loose hay into the hollow. Lying in that hay, wrapped in his blanket and with Floss pressed up against him, he would have been warm enough if he could have had a decent meal inside him.

'It was horrible here yesterday, on my own,' said Fish. I remembered his grey tear-stained face peering over the bales when I first stumbled in, and guessed a little how horrible it must have been in this derelict farm alone, at night, in a snow-storm, utterly lost. 'But now you're here, it's fun,' Fish went on.

Half of me agreed. I was warm and comfortable and full of hot soup, safe and pleasantly tired after my night's adventures. With two of us it *was* rather fun.

The other half of me was not so happy. This half had kept quiet while my tummy was shouting for food, but now it was beginning to take over.

'What are we going to do now?' I asked.

'Have any more sheep been killed?' demanded Fish at once.

I told him about the ones that had been killed at Newbridge.

'Just the once?'

'Just the once.'

Fish was silent, and I knew he was considering. There was something I had to tell him. At the time, it seemed an obvious arrangement; now, seeing Fish still so single-minded and remembering how we had last parted, I was not so sure.

'Were you surprised at seeing me and not Gary?' I asked.

'Not really,' said Fish. 'I thought it would be you.'

'But you told Gary not to tell me.'

'Yeah, but I reckoned he would. He can't get out of his place like you can, or so he says. Anyway, I guessed he'd tell you sooner or later.' He paused, looking sideways at me through the hay. 'I'd have told you, not Gary, anyway, if I'd been able to fix it, honest I would; I just couldn't arrange to meet you.' He got up on one elbow and looked at me, then turned away and stroked Floss. 'No, that's not true,' he said, and his sticky-out ears went all red. It was the first time I had ever known Fish admit, even to himself, that he was telling a lie. 'I'd have been jolly silly to tell you, because all the grown-ups would have been at you, but I expect I would have told you, if it hadn't been for that quarrel.'

'Fish,' I said after thinking back a moment, 'did you always leave that door only half-shut?'

'Only in damp weather. The wood swelled or something, and I was afraid of it sticking with Floss inside.'

'So once she had learnt to push up the latch she could have got out whenever she liked?'

'Yeah,' said Fish. 'I never thought it mattered. After all, she *doesn't* chase sheep.'

He looked at me as though daring me to dispute that fact, but I wasn't that stupid.

'Do you think it is safe for Floss to come home, now?' Fish asked. He sounded so matter-of-fact about it. Did he realize at all, I wondered, just what a to-do there had been over his disappearance? 'Perhaps there's been some more sheep killed since then.' It sounded bad, hoping for sheep to be killed, but I understood how he felt.

'They'll be out hunting for us now, as it is,' I said, and explained my bargain with Gary, and how he would have told my parents what had happened to me when I failed to return this morning. Fish wasn't angry, but he did say he couldn't see that it was exactly a matter of life and death.

'Everybody would think I'd been murdered, like they thought you were,' I said.

'*Murdered?*' said Fish. He was astonished. Such a thought had never entered his head. I realized that the first mention of 'foul play' had been on the early evening news on Wednesday, after Gary had last seen Fish. 'Murdered?' he repeated. 'Who by?' I told him everything that had gone on then, including the bit about his father being held at the police station, and his mother and the girls coming up to our place. I said nothing straightaway about his mum crying in the night, but the first thing Fish said when he had taken it all in was, 'I bet my mum was upset.'

I did tell him then about her crying, but not much. He was silent for a few minutes, then he said,

'I want to go home to my mum.'

'And I do,' I said.

I jumped to my feet and went to the door to see how much snow had fallen.

It *was* deep, really deep. By the doorway Fish and Floss had trampled it down, and because of the strong winds in the night, some of the yard was only covered with a layer a couple of inches thick, but out in the lane it had drifted to two or three feet—more against the straggly hedgerow. It was soft, too. With every step you sank right up to the knees.

I looked at my watch, and it said four-thirty. We were getting near the shortest day, and in another hour it would be almost dark.

We stood in the doorway, and discussed what we would do. It was out of the question to walk all the way home at that

132

hour, or even to Llandewi. There must be farmhouses nearer than Llandewi, probably with telephones, but neither of us had seen one in our midnight wanderings. We had both had too much of getting lost in the night to want to risk doing it again, and we were both very tired still, I from my struggle with the snow last night, Fish from his lonely hazardous life for nearly a week. Somewhere, perhaps not very far away, lay Cwmdu, our proper destination. Presumably, if Gary had told the whole story, a search party had been struggling through the snowdrifts to Cwmdu today. Had they reached it? And, finding it empty, what would they do then?

If they started looking for other buildings, sooner or later they would come to this one, but how soon or how late would depend on how far away we had strayed from Cwmdu. If every lane and track they followed was as full of drifted snow as the one that led to our haven, it could take them days to get to this place, and they had no reason to suppose we were even together.

'What about your bike?' said Fish, suddenly. 'Where did you leave that?'

I had forgotten about the bike. It would be hidden beneath the snow by now, but the search party might have found it.

'If they have stumbled on it by chance,' said Fish, a little too gleefully for my liking, 'they're probably still digging in the snowdrifts in the lane for your dead body.'

I thought of my mum and dad, and Jean and Dan, and poor old Gary. I wouldn't have been in Gary's shoes that day for anything. I turned and sat on the bale by the fire, disconsolately. Fish shut the door and came and joined me.

'We must do something to let them know we're safe,' I said.

'What *can* we do?' asked Fish.

At that moment, Floss whined outside the door. Fish had now blocked up the broken window she had jumped through when she rescued me in the night. He went to let her in and she came and sat in front of us, peacefully licking her wet paws by the dying fire. I went to get some more wood to keep it going; it was obvious we would have to stay for another night at least.

'Couldn't we send a message by Floss?' suggested Fish, when I got back.

'Would she go?' I asked.

'I don't know,' said Fish. 'I half-thought of sending her yesterday, when I couldn't stick it any more; but then I knew I could stick it even less without her, so I didn't try.'

'Could you, Floss?' I asked. She made a great fuss of us both, then, because she knew we were talking about her. She really was a lovely dog—I don't wonder she meant so much to Fish.

'Even if she went, do you think she would find her way? We don't want her to get lost,' I said reluctantly, because it did seem our best chance, but I couldn't let Fish send her off without realizing this could happen.

'She won't get lost, will you, Floss?' said Fish. 'The only thing is, will she agree to leave us?'

'Or know what she is meant to do?' I asked. I thought Floss was a lovely dog, and even a clever dog, but still only a dog, not a superman. 'And if the snow is too much for us, mightn't it be too much for her?'

'You should see her when I go to get water,' said Fish. We decided then we would both go and get water, before it got dark, so we put on our anoraks, nice and dry now, and set out. I could see what Fish meant. It was only twenty yards to the little rivulet, but Floss made it about half a mile, capering round in the snow, doubling away across the hillside and back, burying her nose in the snow and throwing it up in the air, crouching alert, and then galloping in dizzying circles like a mad thing. I've seen other dogs go like that in the snow; it seems to get them that way.

We went back to the farm, and carefully hung our bag of water from a nail.

'What do you think?' asked Fish.

'I vote we try and send her,' I said. 'What message shall we send?' This was a problem. We had no idea what our abandoned farm was called and nothing to write with.

In the end, we decided not to send a message at all. 'Floss will lead them back to us,' said Fish.

'But supposing they don't send her?' I asked. 'Supposing they just think, because Floss has turned up alone, it means you're dead?'

We puzzled over this for a while, and then decided to tie something belonging to each of us to her collar instead—that way they would know we were both alive and both together. But what? We had very little that was recognizably ours that we could spare.

In the end, we laboriously hacked a strip off Fish's blanket with my penknife—Gary would recognize that, because it had once been an army blanket and had a number stamped on one corner—and pulled a bunch of strands from the bobble on my bobble cap—some of each colour.

We were rather pleased with ourselves but it all took time and the light was almost gone before we stood ready at the door with Floss bearing her trophies tied firmly to her collar with wool unravelled from Fish's jersey, and the last of her dog biscuits inside her.

We made a bit of a fuss of Floss, and then Fish said,

'Go on, Floss, go on home. Good dog!' She shot off delightedly, but was back in a flash, inviting us to come with her.

'No,' said Fish. 'We're not coming. You go without us.' Floss sat down patiently and looked up at us. We didn't seem to be doing too well. I tried, but without the slightest success. We began to feel as Sam Morgan must have felt when he tried to make Floss look for us on the mountain-side.

'Home,' said Fish. 'Find Dawn. Where's Dawn gone?' Floss hunted perfunctorily round the yard for Dawn, and came back to say she wasn't there.

'Back to bed,' I said, hopefully. Floss crept meekly by me

into the kitchen and hopped over the bales and sat looking at us over the top. We couldn't help laughing, although it was aggravating, but she really was comical. Then Fish had a brilliant idea.

'Fetch the paper, Floss,' he said, casually, not shouting at all but as though he were standing with her a few yards from the shop.

For one second Floss stared at him as though she couldn't believe her ears. Then she hopped out of bed and went to the door.

'Thanks, Floss. Fetch the paper, then,' said Fish again, very off-hand, as thought it really did not matter.

Floss slipped past us and trotted purposefully across the yard and along the lane. We both followed from a safe distance till we could see round the corner. There went Floss, moving steadily down the lane, over the snow, head up and tail held straight out behind her. We watched her until she melted into the dusk. Then we sighed a little and turned back into the empty kitchen.

Chapter 10

It had suddenly gone very dark. We had been standing looking out at the whiteness of the snow, and so had not noticed
how rapidly the light was going until we came in and shut the
door. The fire glowed a warm and cheerful red in the gloom,
and we went and sat over it.

'This was the horriblest time yesterday,' said Fish. 'I had
meant to have a rest and then set out for Cwmdu, or help, or
something. Then it suddenly got dark, like this, and I
thought, it's too late to go anywhere; I'd have to stay here. I'd
collected in some of this brushwood, thinking I'd light a fire,
and then I discovered the matches were all wet. It was dark,
and cold, and spooky, and there was nothing for me to do
except lie down and go to sleep, and I *couldn't* sleep.' I looked
at my watch, but it was already much too dark to read it. I
held it to the glow of the fire, peering at it, but it wasn't easy.

'Fire wants making up,' I said.

'Let's light a candle, too,' said Fish.

He burrowed in the bag for one, and lit it, while I got some
more wood and built up the fire. I looked again at my watch in
the candlelight, and it was half past six.

'What shall we do now?' I asked. The candle and the fire
only cast a little light, and the dark corners of the room
seemed even darker by comparison. The bare window put me
off a bit. 'Let's shut the spooks out,' I said, and started looking around for something to cover it with. Eventually I peeled
a large strip of ancient wallpaper off one wall—it was hanging
in shreds anyway—and tried to wedge it in place with some
brushwood. It wasn't very successful, but it was a slight im-
provement.

137

'Do you know what I'd like?' said Fish. 'A lovely hot bath.'

'Don't,' I said. 'I'd even quite enjoy cleaning my teeth.'

'We could pretend,' said Fish, hopefully. 'Our bed looks quite like a bath.' We went and sat in it, facing each other, pretending to scrub ourselves, and making bubbles, and playing with imaginary boats, and making jokes about the water being too hot.

'Shall I pull the plug out now?' asked Fish.

'Hm,' I said, after a moment. 'The water isn't running away very fast.'

'Too dirty, I expect,' said Fish.

He was right, there. The first bath we got into would be about as thick as hay by the time we had washed all the dirt off us. Fish had more layers on than me, I suppose, because he had spent longer collecting it, but I didn't feel exactly clean. For one thing, though lying in hay is lovely when you are dead tired, you get to feel all tickly after a bit.

'I suppose we *could* go and wash in the stream,' I said doubtfully. Fish shivered. 'Are you mad?' he asked. 'Pity there's nothing bigger than a soup packet to heat water in.'

'There might be,' I said. 'Nothing we can cook food in, but there might be an old saucepan or bucket or something lying around in one of the outbuildings. It would do to wash in.'

We took the torch and went exploring. Fish had already been upstairs, but I hadn't, so that was where we started. At the top there were just two little empty rooms, with rotten floorboards and broken windows. As I swung the beam of light into the second room a white shape suddenly flitted noiselessly out of the darkness and disappeared. Then it shrieked eerily outside, and was gone.

After five seconds I knew it was a barn owl, but for those five seconds I learnt the real meaning of the expression 'scared stiff'. I could move neither arm nor leg, I wanted to scream but my jaw was rigid and no sound came from my throat; even the very blood stood still in my veins. Then Fish clutched me.

138

'What was that?' he whispered. He had been behind me, so had actually seen nothing. All he had heard was the shriek.

'Only an owl,' I whispered back, fiercely. I hoped Fish thought I was fierce with him for sounding frightened, but in truth I was speaking to myself.

'It made a funny noise,' said Fish, humbly.

'Barn owls always sound like that,' I said. 'Come on, there's nothing here. Let's go down again.' I did not want Fish to see how I was shaking.

He turned and stumbled down the dark stairs ahead of me, and went to the door.

'Let's go round the outhouses, then,' he said. 'There's more likely to be something there.'

'Let's not bother,' I said. It takes a bit of time to get over being as scared as that.

'It's all very well for you,' said Fish. 'You probably had a bath only a couple of days ago, and anyway, you *like* being dirty. I want a hot wash.' And he took the torch and clambered out through the snow. There was nothing for me to do but follow, because I would rather have his company than be by myself in the flickering firelight.

It was a fruitless hunt. All we found was one very battered enamel pan, such as the farmer's wife might have used once to take feed out to the hens, and that had a hole in the bottom. However, we took it in with us; Fish thought we might be able to block up the hole, but I didn't see how.

To tell the truth, I was beginning to feel pretty depressed. When I had first woken up, and we got the fire going and cooked our meal, I was so happy to be warm again, and rested and safe, that I felt on top of the world, and so had Fish. Now the steam was beginning to go out of the adventure for me. I could only think of all the worry and misery at home today, and the trouble I would be in tomorrow. Boys in adventure stories go tearing off on adventures quite like ours, but always seem to return home with enough hidden treasure or unmasked crooks to be able to buy off their parents' anger; but what had we to show? We were not even sure that Floss had proved her innocence.

I did not say any of this to Fish. He was still full of life—it was such a treat for him to have company again, and I began to admire him a lot for sticking it out by himself for so long. As I sat gloomily on the bale in front of the fire Fish fussed around putting on more wood and looking for things to mend his pan with.

'Hi!' said Fish suddenly. 'Come and look at this. What's this tap for?' He was standing beside the fire.

'I don't know,' I answered. 'But I've seen a fire-place like

140

this before, at my auntie's. I think it's what they call an old kitchen range. People used to cook on them somehow. Perhaps that was an oven.'

'Funny sort of oven,' said Fish. 'Got no door. Could be one on the other side, though.' I came over and had a look.

The fire-place was set in a wide space, which was filled up with a sort of black iron box on each side. The one on the left could, as Fish said, have been an oven, but the one on the right had no door, only a tap, and a round lid on the top.

'It's got a lid,' I said. 'Don't touch it—it'll burn you,' I cried as Fish made as though to pick it up by the knob on top.

'Do you suppose you poured rice pudding in at the top and it ran out through the tap?' asked Fish, giggling.

'Don't be daft,' I said. 'It's more likely it was for heating water.' I said it without thinking.

'For heating water?' repeated Fish.

'Most likely,' I said, stupidly. 'But there won't be any in now.'

'*There soon can be, though,*' said Fish—and only then did I get the point.

'To think,' I said, 'that we've been spending all this time looking for some sort of pan, and we can heat all the water we want in that thing.'

'That's right,' said Fish. 'You get the lid off, and I'll bring the water.' He went off with his polythene bag to the stream, and I wrestled with the lid. It wasn't at all easy, because it was so hot, and rusted in as well. I still hadn't succeeded when Fish returned, so we raked the fire, which was fairly low again by now, to the other side of the grate and splashed some water on the embers next to the boiler, and on the top of the boiler itself. It fairly sizzled and steamed, and I scalded the side of my hand, which made me very angry and go hopping round the room almost crying with the pain. However, eventually the lid came off, and Fish poured in the rest of his water, which made more sizzlings and steam than ever. Actually,

141

when I told Dad about this part later on, he said that it was desperately dangerous to light a big fire alongside an empty boiler, or to pour cold water into it while the fire was alight, and he could not think why we had not both been blown to kingdom come. That may have been so, but we knew nothing about all that at the time, so it did not worry us—yet I still wake up in a sweat sometimes from nightmares about that white owl in the upstairs room, though there was never a shadow of danger from the poor bird, and probably wouldn't have been even if it had been a real ghost.

'We'll need lots more water,' said Fish. 'I don't suppose that lot even reaches the level of the tap.'

'Isn't there a better way?' I asked. I could see Fish traipsing back and forth to the stream with his polythene bag all night.

Fish looked about the room. 'If you stayed here, I could use your wellingtons,' he said doubtfully.

'Thank *you*,' I remarked sarcastically. 'I'd rather use yours.'

'What about snow?' suggested Fish. That seemed a good idea, until we tried it. Apart from the fact that it takes an awful lot of snow to make a tiny amount of water, we found it cold and miserable plodding in and out through the open door with the enamel pan—at least we found a use for that—looking for snow that had not been trampled on, and then trying to insert it though the small round hole at the top of the boiler. So much rubbed off and ran down the side into the grate that we nearly put our fire out, and what little did go in was black from the sides of the opening.

Then I had a bright idea. 'Why not use your duffle bag?' I said. It had a waterproof lining, would soon dry out afterwards, and though it might leak a bit it would hold so much that we could afford to lose some. Once it had been full of Fish's stores. Now it was quite empty—no, not quite empty, because when Fish tipped it upside-down, out fell a piece of soap!

'Why, I'd quite forgotten I'd got that,' said Fish. 'I did all my washing at Bottom Barn without any.'

'We are obviously meant to have a good wash tonight,' I said. We went out together, then, with the duffle bag, and filled it to the brim. It was surprising how heavy it was to carry home, but it filled the boiler at least half full, and that was good enough for us.

That done, we settled down to cook the rest of the soup for our supper while the water heated. As Fish said, we were bound to get mucky cooking so we might as well leave washing till the last thing. I suppose at the back of both our minds was the thought that a rescue party might walk in at any time during the night, and we felt we would make a better impression if we were reasonably clean.

We used both the remaining packets of soup. It was easier now we had an extra empty packet to mix it in, and we were hungry again. By the morning, if we were not rescued, we decided we should set out straightaway ourselves, and not waste time lighting fires again. We ate everything except for one packet of biscuits and one bar of chocolate.

Then we washed, using the duffle bag as a wash-basin. The water was lovely and hot, and the room was warm, too. Fish stripped off everything and really got down to it, and when he remembered we had no towel he danced upon the bale in front of the fire to dry himself, singing and acting the fool. So then I stripped, too, and washed and danced on the other bale, and soon felt really cheerful again.

'Where's my striped pyjamas?' sang Fish. 'Must have a clean pair,' and he pulled on his filthy old jeans.

'Oh, I've lost my bedroom slippers, I've lost my bedroom slippers, I've lost my bedroom slippers—so I'll wear my wellies instead,' I sang, clumping back into my boots.

'I hope you're not going to wear those in bed,' said Fish. 'Must clean my teeth,' and he went to the door and rubbed his teeth with snow. I did the same—it was a nice refreshing feeling, and I felt quite as though it were a normal bed-time. I

even said my prayers automatically at the bale-side before hopping in and rolling up in the blanket with Fish.

We pulled the loose hay over us, but there was one thing missing—the comfortable warm weight of a dog.

'I wonder where Floss has got to,' said Fish. We were quiet then, and the bright spirits ebbed away. I watched the fire-light flickering on the peeling wallpaper, and in my mind's eye pictured Floss bravely ploughing through the snow, bent for the village shop.

'Do you think she will get tired and come back half-way?' I said.

'No,' said Fish, 'but I'm wondering what will happen if she gets there in the middle of the night and nobody is around to see her.'

'Somebody will be around,' I said. 'They'll be looking for us.' And my heart sank again as I said it; there would be no sleep for my mother or father tonight, and tomorrow I would have to explain myself.

'I hope she doesn't get run over,' said Fish.

'Why should she?' I asked. 'She never has done.'

'No,' said Fish. But he was still worried.

All the same, we were warm, clean, fed, and tired. Eventually we both dropped off to sleep, some time before midnight.

When we woke in the morning the fire had gone out and the room was cold. I became conscious that it was daylight and opened my eyes, to see Fish just rousing himself too. I was sleepily wondering why we had both woken up at the same time, when I heard a noise, and knew in a strange kind of way that the noise had been going on earlier and that was what had awakened us. It was something scratching at the door.

'Listen!' I said. For a moment Fish lay still, as still as I was, but when the scratching came again he laughed and jumped out of bed.

'I know who that is,' he said, and ran and opened the door.

In came Floss, wet and bedraggled, but grinning and lashing her tail about—and in her mouth she carried Fish's favourite comic!

She handed the paper over to Fish and then bounded into bed with us, making a great fuss of us, and we of her—and yet we did not know whether to laugh or cry.

Neither of us had known quite what would happen when we sent Floss back to the village, or how help would come back to us, but the one thing that had never crossed our minds was that Floss would simply do as she was told and come back to us with the paper, without arousing any response from the people back at home.

'Surely Mrs Burns didn't just *give* her the paper and think no more about it?' I asked.

'Shouldn't think so,' said Fish absently. I saw that something on the back page of the comic had caught his eye.

'Look, Fish,' I said impatiently, 'you can't sit and read your comic *now*.'

'I don't see why not,' he said. 'Floss has gone to a lot of trouble to bring it.'

He sounded so cool. 'You're daft,' I said. 'We ought to be doing something.'

'Yeah,' he said. 'Giving Floss some biscuits.' He got up and rummaged around till he found the rest of our food supply. 'Hang on to those a minute. I'll just get her a drink.' He ran some water out of the boiler, now cold, into the duffle bag, and offered it to Floss. She drank deeply, and then jumped back on top of me in bed and began to nuzzle hopefully at the packet of biscuits in my hand.

'What do you suppose can have happened?' I asked, uneasily.

'Can't think,' said Fish. 'But those things round her neck have gone. Look!' That was true, but did that mean someone had taken them off, or that they had been torn off as she pushed through a hedgerow?

I asked Fish what he thought, but he just said, 'Come on; let's divide up the biscuits. We might as well have breakfast in bed—it's cold out there.' He nodded at the room, looking bleak in the morning light, with the dead ashes in the hearth.

'As soon as we've had breakfast we had better set out for home,' I said. 'I wonder what the snow is like? I think I'll just go and see.'

'Oh, stop worrying,' said Fish. 'Floss is safely back, and that's the main thing.' And so it was, for Fish. His eye was already straying back to the comic, as he helped himself to a biscuit and started munching absently. I climbed out and went across to the window. There was still a lot of snow about, but no more than yesterday. It would not be easy walking, but we had the day before us and it could be done. After all, we would only have to get as far as Llandewi-fach to find someone with a telephone—there was no need to walk all the twelve miles home.

Fish was right. Our best course was to stay quietly in bed and eat breakfast, and let Floss have a well-earned rest, before we set out. As I climbed back into our hay-filled haven, Fish's hand and Floss's nose came out exploring for the biscuit packet which I still held in my hand. I stooped to retrieve the old enamel pan and put one-third of the biscuits into it, for Floss. The rest I divided in two, giving half to Fish. As I began to eat my share, Fish started laughing over some joke in his paper. I settled down beside him and looked over his shoulder to see what he was laughing at. Soon we were both absorbed, sitting side by side and silently turning the pages from time to time. Floss sat at our feet and licked herself.

And that was how my father, and Sam, and Mr Thomas, found us when they walked in five minutes later.

Chapter 11

'WELL, I'll be . . .' said Mr Thomas.

My father and Sam just looked at us in silence, and we were silent, too. Fish recovered first.

'Would you like a biscuit?' he asked nervously.

'Ta,' said Sam.

'Got a cup o' tea to go with it?' asked Mr Thomas, sarcastically.

'I'm afraid not,' said Fish. 'But if you'd like to sit down'—he waved at the two bales in front of the hearth—'we can soon light the fire. I expect you're a bit wet,' he added politely.

I looked at Dad, and he looked at me, and neither of us could speak. He came and sat on the bale at the edge of the bed, and I climbed out and sat beside him.

Mr Thomas lowered himself on to the bale and stretched his legs out slowly in front of him. Then he reached into his trouser pocket and pulled out a pipe. Fish proceeded to put wisps of hay and brushwood on to the hot ash, not really quite sure what he was doing, but in a moment it began to smoulder of its own accord. Sam had gone to the door and was talking into a walkie-talkie that he had been carrying.

'Yes,' he was saying. 'Both of them. Safe and sound. . . . No, I don't think so.' He turned to us. 'Any injuries?' he said.

'I burnt my finger,' said Fish. He waved it in the air. Sam looked across at me, and I shook my head. There wasn't anything to show where I had scalded my hand, although it did feel a bit sore.

'No,' said Sam, into the machine. 'They were having break-

fast in bed reading a comic when we arrived. Yes. No, haven't gone into all that yet. You tell their mothers they're both fine.' He switched it off and came back in.

'Your mother's been very worried about you,' said Dad, quietly. It was the first time he had spoken.

I looked across at his hands, because I dared not look up at his face, trying to see if he was angry. I swallowed a couple of times.

'I know,' I said at last. 'I'm sorry.'

'It were that bike,' said Dad. 'That bike in the snow.'

'Did you find that?' I asked.

Sam told us then what had happened, with Mr Thomas chipping in. Dad said nothing at all.

149

Because yesterday had been Saturday, nobody had discovered I was missing till after eleven o'clock in the morning. Mum had called up to me once or twice, but she just thought I was over-tired after all the excitement of the week, and that it would do me good to have a lie-in. Gary no doubt was in a great state of nerves, but he could not very well come up to our place to see if I was all right. It would look odd, especially through all that snow. However, in the end he did just that. Mum greeted him cheerfully and told him to go on up and wake me. Poor old Gary! He must have guessed then what had happened.

Afterwards he told me how he sat on my empty bed for what seemed hours, staring out at the blanket of snow through which he had struggled to get to the Rhos, plucking up courage to go and tell my mum about it.

As soon as she began to grasp what it was all about, my mother shouted for Dad to get the tractor out. There wasn't a hope of getting the van down the snow-filled lane. She loaded Dawn and Dan into the box at the back with Jean to look after them, and set off herself with Gary in the wake of the lurching tractor down to Tygwyn, stopping at the Ferns to tell the Barneses about Fish. For them it was the first good news of the week. Mr Barnes started on down with Gary and Mum straightaway, and his wife followed soon after with Tracy.

Gary told his story all over again to Mr Barnes, and then to his father, and then to Sam, and then to I don't know how many other policemen. He was saved the reporters at that time because the village was still cut off from the outside world by the snow. The snow-plough that had started work on the main road was at once diverted on to the mountain road to Llandewi, and another was called in to work on the lanes up to Cwmdu. Meantime they had got a Land-rover as far as the first right-hand fork after Llandewi, and from there Mr Thomas and my father led a party on foot through the snow-choked lanes to Cwmdu.

They found Cwmdu deserted and shuttered, as it had been

left at the end of the summer, just at the same time as the snow-plough, working over the ridge, had shovelled up Tom's bike. They radioed the news through to Sam who had got his walkie-talkie at Cwmdu, and they plodded gloomily back to the spot, Sam prodding the deeper drifts with a stick as they went along. They knew now that *I* was somewhere in the area, but nobody had any idea where Fish could be. By this time it was late afternoon, and the light was going.

'Didn't you meet Floss on the road?' asked Fish. It was a long time between sending Floss off at half past five and her triumphant return at nine o'clock in the morning.

Apparently two policemen, working at the spot where the bicycle had been found, *had* seen Floss. She slipped by them purposefully in the gloom, and they thought little about it. They were not local men, and did not recognize her. Mr Thomas and Sam and my father were all exploring the side lanes, but not, as it happened, the ones that Floss followed, and they never got as far as our hide-out before total darkness fell, and further search was useless. They went home wearily in the Land-rover.

At about nine o'clock that evening Mr Thomas saw a light across the valley. He called his oldest son, Kevin, and they ran over to investigate. But it was only old Williams of Aberdulais, still worrying about the sheep attacks. He was armed with his rifle and a powerful torch, and he had heard some bleating up on the hillside above. They talked in low voices in the darkness for a while, and then the sheep in the field they were standing in began to bleat and stampede in the darkness.

Old Williams handed the torch to Kevin. 'You swing that around, boy, and if you get any dog in the beam, just you keep it on him; I'll soon settle him.'

Kevin did so, sweeping the beam over the huddled sheep with their green slit eyes and across the upper field. There, moving stealthily along below the hedge, was a dog.

Quick as a flash, Williams raised his gun, and fired, but Mr

Thomas was quicker. He thrust the barrel sideways with a sudden blow, and Williams swung round angrily.

'What the . . .?' he exclaimed.

'That dog wasn't after sheep. That was Floss!' cried Mr Thomas. And he ran across the field, followed by Kevin, calling Floss by name, while Williams was left alone in the dark spluttering and swearing. He lived on his own, taking little interest in local affairs and, though of course he knew about the missing boy, the name Floss meant nothing particular to him.

Floss had disappeared. There had been no sound, so they assumed she had not been hit, but she could well have been frightened away. When they got to the lane there was still no sign of her, so they turned towards the village as that was the direction in which she had been heading. Mr Thomas was getting puffed, and slowed to a walk, but Kevin jogged on into the village, and as he came within sight of the nearer of the two street lights the first thing he saw was Floss trotting peacefully along the snowy road in front of him. When she got to the village shop, she stopped and sat down in front of the door.

Kevin ran up to her. She was, as always, delighted to see him, and made no move to run away. She jumped up, and wagged her tail, and rolled on the ground; but when he started to walk back towards his father, she sat down again outside the shop.

Keeping a wary eye on her, he went and knocked on Sam's door, which was only twenty yards away. Sam came out just as Mr Thomas appeared, panting, on the scene, and together they told their story. Having found the things still tied round Floss's neck, they took her straight up to Tygwyn, where all my family were spending the night, so as to be within reach of the telephone. Gary identified the blanket, and my mother the wool from my bobble hat. It was a great moment, according to Mr Thomas. Here, for the first time, was some proof, not only that we were both alive but that we were together.

Floss enjoyed the fuss and drank the milk Mrs Thomas gave her, but she did not eat anything and seemed anxious and restless. It was my mother who said they ought to let her go, and follow her.

Time, however, was important, or so they thought, and they knew from the abandoned bicycle that I had got well beyond Llandewi. It seemed a waste of time to follow Floss on foot all that way, when maybe every minute counted. My father and Sam and Mr Thomas got into the Land-rover, taking Floss with them, leaving Kevin to go over to the Ferns with the news, and they drove straight up to the place where the bicycle had been found.

'Good dog, then,' said Sam. 'Where's your master?' Floss did not hesitate. She turned straight round and trotted back towards Llandewi-fach.

At this point in the story, Fish began to giggle because he guessed what was going to happen. Floss led the mystified party straight back through Llandewi, and on down the mountain road back into Llanwern. When she got to the village shop once more, she sat down again outside the door. She must have been very tired by then, but no more so than the worried and frustrated trio who had followed her. By this time it was four o'clock in the morning.

It was Mrs Burns herself who solved the problem. The voices outside woke her up, and she stuck her head out of her bedroom window to find out what was going on. Sam started to explain and Mrs Burns wrapped herself in her dressing-gown and came down to the door. As soon as she opened it, Floss trotted inside and stood on her hind legs in front of the counter.

'Paper, Floss?' said Mrs Burns, at four o'clock in the morning, as though it were the most natural thing in the world. 'There you are, then.' And she took down a copy of Fish's favourite comic, folded it and put it in Floss's mouth. 'Taking it back to your master, is it?' asked Mrs Burns. She will swear to this day that Floss actually nodded, but my dad

153

thinks Mrs Burns imagined that bit. In any event, Floss turned round and set off once more over the bridge and up the hill road to Llandewi-fach.

'Well, I'll be . . .' said Mr Thomas, on that occasion, too.

They had left the Land-rover up by the bicycle, so while my father plodded up the hill after Floss, Sam and Mr Thomas went to borrow another one. When they caught up with my father Floss got in willingly enough, and they all drove as far as Llandewi.

They were more cautious this time. At Llandewi they stopped and put Floss out to see which way she went. Then they picked her up again and proceeded to the first turning, and so on until they came to the bicycle place.

From then on they followed her on foot, but both dog and men were pretty exhausted by that time and they made slow progress. It was only over the last mile that Floss picked up speed again, and then she left them behind, but they could follow her tracks, which were easily visible in the snow. That was how they came to be ten minutes behind when she scratched at our door.

There's not much more to tell, really, except for one thing that everybody had forgotten about except Fish.

'Thank you,' he said, very seriously, to Mr Thomas, 'thank you for saving Floss's life.' He turned to me. 'We should never have sent her,' he said. 'I never thought she might get shot.'

He looked round the little room that had become his home. 'If it's not safe for Floss down there, I'm not coming back. I'm staying here.'

Well, it was a daft thing to say, but it was brave, and he meant it.

Sam laughed, but kindly. 'There's no need for you to worry,' he said. 'When we went up to Pugh's to borrow his Land-rover, he'd just shot a dog that he'd caught actually at his sheep. An old one, it was, that's been seen around up on the hills; gone wild, they say, and living off the land. Probably been around for months. I reckon that's the end of sheep-killing in our district for a good long while.'

'Then you don't think it ever was Floss?'

'No, sonny.' He looked at Floss, asleep flat out before the fire. 'I reckon she's training for the marathon at the next Olympics. She ain't got no time for sheep-chasing.'

'But you did think so, once, didn't you?' persisted Fish.

'I never thought there was enough evidence to take action,' said Sam, judicially.

Fish looked at him. 'Dad did,' he said.

Sam looked embarrassed. 'Yes, well,' he said. 'He won't think so now, though.'

Mr Thomas spoke up then. 'Your Floss is a dog any man can be proud of,' he said, 'and when we tell your father the whole story I fancy he'll be as proud of Floss as anybody.'

He was, and in a funny way he was proud of Fish, too. I was worried for Fish, but I need not have been. Mr Barnes treated Fish much more like a grown-up person, and instead of making me feel uncomfortable by making much of me in front of Fish he took to boasting about Fish in front of me. I didn't mind, though. Fish and I were pretty good friends by now, and what Mr Barnes thought did not count much one way or the other as far as I was concerned. I don't know how Fish felt about his father after our adventure, because he never talked about him. But he was mighty glad to get back to his mum—and I guess she was pretty happy to have him back, too.

When all the explanations were over, we walked back to the Land-rovers. Dad and I were in front at one time, and after we had walked in silence for a long while, I said, cautiously, 'Are you very angry, Dad?'

He did not answer for a long time. Then he said, 'Tell you what; if you'd told me about Floss that very first evening when we lost our sheep, it would have been honest, and it would have saved an awful lot of bother, because I could have seen, then, that he kept that dog shut up at night, proper. But since you didn't, and things got the way they did, well, I'm not saying as if I'd been you I'd have acted any different.'

And that was all he ever said on the subject. But later that evening, when we'd all got back to Tygwyn and all the families had been reunited, and Mum had done hugging me and started laying into me instead, when Dan was having supper and Jean was reading and Mum was standing by the sink going on at me, Dad looked up from the armchair in the corner where he was sitting and winked at me; and then we all started laughing.